He—Loukas Ari... window with his... room.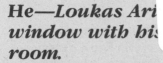

As she studied his silhouette, that other image of him, which she had carried around in her head for weeks, dispersed like smoke into the warm air.

He looked taller, broader, than he had last evening. This man was as different from her stereotypical idea, formed through long experience, of a publicity-shy, introverted art collector and historian as it was possible to be. Black jeans hugged his slim hips and a white linen shirt stretched across the width of his shoulders.

Sophia's fingers curled more tightly around the edges of her laptop. She braced both knees and mentally adjusted her approach to this project. She had the feeling it was going to be unlike any other one she'd ever undertaken. This man, with his dark eyes and air of solemnity, intrigued her. But her interest, and that of Marshalls, lay with his collection. That was what she needed to concentrate on...

Dear Reader,

Exploring the Aegean Sea, it's not difficult to imagine meeting a character from *The Odyssey* on the ancient stones of a harbor wall, but when Sophia Shaw arrives on Loukas Ariti's private island to value his art collection, she finds herself in the middle of a very modern Greek tragedy.

Betrayal and loss have shaped Loukas into a man who will never allow himself to love. Sophia, forced by a devastating injury to abandon her career as a ballet dancer, has faced trauma with courage and hope.

Will she be able to unlock Loukas's emotions and enable him to love her, or must she leave him to his life of solitude and try to move on?

When Loukas reveals a shocking truth, her decision is made, but leaving is never easy if your heart remains behind.

I once spent a blissful summer island-hopping around Greece, falling in love with the rugged, volcanic landscapes and Homer's "wine-dark seas." I hope you will find some of their magic in Sophia and Loukas's story of loss, hope and the ultimate power of love.

Suzanne

Ballerina and the Greek Billionaire

Suzanne Merchant

ISBN-13: 978-1-335-59641-3

Ballerina and the Greek Billionaire

Copyright © 2023 by Suzanne Merchant

Recycling programs
for this product may
not exist in your area.

For questions and comments about the quality of this book, please contact us at CustomerService@Harlequin.com.

Harlequin Enterprises ULC
22 Adelaide St. West, 41st Floor
Toronto, Ontario M5H 4E3, Canada
www.Harlequin.com

Printed in U.S.A.

Suzanne Merchant was born and raised in South Africa. She and her husband lived and worked in Cape Town, London, Kuwait, Baghdad, Sydney and Dubai before settling in the Sussex countryside. They enjoy visits from their three grown-up children and are kept busy attempting to wrangle two spaniels, a dachshund, a parrot and a large, unruly garden under control.

Books by Suzanne Merchant

Harlequin Romance

Their Wildest Safari Dream
Off-Limits Fling with the Billionaire

Visit the Author Profile page
at Harlequin.com.

For Tom, remembering our island-hopping summer.

CHAPTER ONE

HE HADN'T PLANNED for this.

Loukas Ariti, billionaire and reluctant visitor to his own private island, leaned forward, giving himself a better view from the window.

When his helicopter pilot had dropped him off on Alysos yesterday, the memories, which he'd tried to keep locked away for most of his life, had shattered the restraints he'd forced on them, and broken free. They'd come at him from all sides, escaping from his own personal Pandora's box, taking him hostage.

He was counting the days—the *hours*—until he could leave again, and never, ever return.

The Aegean had darkened to deep blue in the late afternoon light, and the shadows, black and sharp at midday, were softening and lengthening. Skiathos lay to the west, its outline dissolving in the dusk, but Loukas's attention was fixed on something closer.

Marshalls Auction House had undertaken to send him their most skilful art historian. The director had been so keen to secure this contract that Loukas felt sure he would have thrown in the Mona Lisa if he'd demanded it. At least, he thought, the man should have come himself.

He'd been at this window, watching Stephanos bring the *Athena* in, from the time the boat had been a tiny dot, skimming over the waves, until he'd tied her up at the quayside and helped his passenger ashore. He narrowed his eyes against the low rays of the sun to focus on the small figure climbing the rocky track towards his door.

The skirt of the woman's summer dress swung below her knees, and she carried a laptop bag over one shoulder. As she climbed nearer, her pace slowing, he could see that her hair hung, sleek and golden, to her shoulders, cut in a sharp-edged bob.

She paused for a moment, looked up at the house, then set off again at a more modest pace.

He sighed. The idea of a stranger under the roof of his long-dead godfather's villa was almost impossible to imagine. The idea that the stranger might be a beautiful young woman was just about intolerable. It reminded him of that fateful summer, thirty years ago.

Not that he needed reminding.

He pulled back from the window and headed towards the door.

Sophia stopped, slipped the bag off her shoulder and planted her fists on her hips. She drew in a couple of deep breaths, her heart hammering, and wished she'd set herself a slower pace.

This morning, a crispness in the London air had hinted at the arrival of autumn, but the Greek sun still shone with warmth, even in the late afternoon.

The man who had piloted the insanely fast and slick speedboat that had brought her from Skiathos was still on the quayside, along with her carry-on bag. That boat—the *Athena*—lay at the stone quay, rising and falling on the gentle swell. Sophia had clung to the polished rail at her side when the pilot—he'd introduced himself as Stephanos—had opened up the throttle and headed out of the harbour. The curved bow had lifted from the water as they'd gained speed, waves thudding against the hull. She'd watched as the island of Skiathos shrank into the distance behind them, and mentally cast her fate into Neptune's hands.

She was about to meet the famously private owner of a collection, the possible value of which had caused wild speculation in the world of fine art. It was said no outsider had viewed it for thirty years. The owner's decision to sell was a mystery, but when he'd approached Marshalls, they'd jumped at the chance to catalogue and sell the contents of the house on this island. It could legitimately be dubbed the sale of the century, if they succeeded in bringing the collection to auction. And it all depended on her.

The well-used, annotated copy of a guide to the Islands of the Aegean, which she'd found amongst her grandfather's books, had intrigued her. His love of Greek and Roman art and sculpture had rubbed off on her, and his expertise in the subject had been respected in the art world, but evidence that her grandparents had frequently travelled to Greece had been unexpected.

They'd never talked to her about holidays they'd taken before she was born. They'd never really talked to her about anything at all.

So when her boss had suggested that she was the person for this job she'd been filled with excitement.

She relished the challenge. Life had taught her, the hard way, that the only person she could depend on was herself, and she was confident enough of her capabilities to believe she could manage the assignment.

The house clung to the slopes of the rocky hill above her. Sophia's impression was of dazzling white walls, tiles and shutters the colour of the sky, and the extravagant scramble of magenta bougainvillea. She shouldered her bag again and, setting her jaw, launched herself at the final flight of steps.

A polished brass lion's head, a ring clutched between its teeth, adorned the weathered oak of the door. She gripped the ring, the smoothness of decades of use caressing her palm. But before she could knock, the door swung inwards.

'Oh…' Her surprise at the door opening was instantly eclipsed by the impact of the man who stood in front of her.

Even allowing for her own petite frame and height, he was tall, she thought. Very tall. And built, although not in an aggressive, pumped-up way. He'd look as at home on the deck of a racing yacht, or on a downhill ski run, as he would pounding a treadmill or lifting weights in a gym. He was rather different from the academics she'd grown used to dealing with in her role as a cataloguer and valuer of art.

The man she had come to see was intensely private. She knew that. And she knew his name. He appeared to have no social media presence and no discoverable footprint. Therefore, the man in front of her, in hip-hugging jeans and a linen shirt, sleeves rolled to the elbows, bronzed, sockless feet in worn boat shoes, was not, could not be, Loukas Ariti.

Perhaps, she thought, he was a bodyguard, someone who stood between the shadowy collector and the rest of the world, protecting his life and shielding his privacy. That would account for his grim expression and the dark eyes that scrutinised her, expertly assessing the level of threat she posed. He nodded once and moved back a pace. No threat, then, Sophia thought, ruefully.

She stepped over the threshold into a dim hall and put out her hand.

'Sophia Shaw. From Marshalls? I'm here to see Mr Ariti...'

He closed the door behind her, shutting out the light, and she dropped her hand, smoothing it over her right thigh. Her palm was damp, and she knew the exertion of her climb was not solely responsible, but she squashed the little twist of anxiety that had suddenly tightened in her stomach.

She lifted her chin and met his stare.

'You are the top researcher your boss—Sean?— promised to send?'

Sophia held his gaze. 'Yes, I am,' she said.

He nodded. Perhaps the slight roughness in his voice meant he hadn't spoken for a while. Perhaps he believed in silence as well as solitude. But beneath the huskiness ran a note as smooth as dark chocolate, even though it looked as if smiling was an exercise he'd have to study and consider carefully, before trying it out.

She proffered her hand again and this time he took it, briefly enclosing it in a warm, dry grip.

'Loukas Ariti.'

'I'm pleased to meet you, Mr Ariti.' She replaced her hand on the strap of her laptop bag. 'So you're not the bodyguard, after all?'

'*Bodyguard?* Why...?'

Sophia smiled up at him but there was no answering flicker in the corner of the stern, straight line of his mouth.

'Oh, it's just that you don't look like someone who has spent the last thirty years avoiding publicity and curating an art collection.'

'That's because I haven't. That is, I may have kept out of the public eye, but I haven't curated the collection.'

'I thought perhaps the person who *has* curated it was locked away in his study.'

'And I was protecting him.' He nodded. 'I see. And for the record, *I* didn't know who Marshalls' top researcher was, either. I didn't read the details of Sean's email. I just knew someone was arriving today. How was your journey?'

Sophia exhaled and dropped her shoulders.

'Um…okay, thank you. Long. I left…'

But if he'd had any interest at all in her answer, he appeared to have lost it already. He turned, inclining his dark head in an invitation to follow him, and strode away down a passage.

Sophia hitched her laptop bag higher onto her shoulder and followed. Tension stiffened his wide shoulders, the muscles taut beneath the fine blue-and-white-striped cloth of his shirt. His thick black slightly too long hair curled just above the collar.

'I… Oh, my goodness!'

He'd walked ahead of her through a wide arch,

and stepped aside, and Sophia found herself gazing at one of the most breathtaking views she'd ever seen. Sliding glass doors were pushed back to either side, leaving most of one wall open. Beyond was a marble terrace, wrapped around on three sides by wings of the house. The fourth side was occupied by an infinity pool, which lay like a burnished mirror, reflecting the pink rays of the sinking sun. Further away, the darkening sea melted into the sky, where the bright jewel of Venus shone, solitary and splendid, not yet in competition with the light from millions of stars.

Sophia took a few steps towards the terrace.

'This is…more than beautiful. It's…perfect.' She breathed in, relishing the scent from the thyme and lavender that grew in a collection of terracotta pots. Then, remembering the man who wasn't the bodyguard but Loukas Ariti himself, she half turned towards him and saw that he'd been joined by an elderly, grey-haired woman who stood half a pace behind him, with her hands clasped in front of her. She was dressed in black, her eyes bright with interest as she studied Sophia.

'This is Anna.' That voice, husky and deep, pulled Sophia's attention back to him. 'She will take care of anything you need during your stay.' He pushed long fingers through his untidy hair and flexed his shoulders. His attitude radiated unease, as if he could hardly wait to leave the room.

'She will show you to your accommodation and serve you dinner.'

'Thank you.' Sophia smiled at them both. 'I'm keen to begin work. Will I be able to start this evening?'

He shook his head and frowned. 'No. You must be tired after your journey. You can begin in the morning, but I'd like the task to be accomplished as quickly as possible.'

He turned away and moved back towards the archway. Sophia now noticed it was flanked by smooth marble columns. A bronze statue of a ballerina stood on a low table nearby. She recognised the work of a well-known sculptor.

'There're procedures I need to discuss with you, before beginning.' He was about to be engulfed in the shadows of the passage and she was anxious to establish at least a few facts before he vanished.

He stopped, hesitated, then turned back to her, dipping his head, his face a study in planes and angles, his mouth a firm line beneath a strong, slightly roman nose.

'Naturally, Miss Shaw. Please meet me in my study at nine o'clock tomorrow morning. Anna will show you the way.' He nodded. 'Good evening.'

Loukas closed the study door and leaned against its reassuring solidity. He tipped his head back and shut his eyes, exhaling an unsteady breath.

Even though he'd been longing for this day, it was proving so much harder than he'd expected, and he had braced himself for the worst.

Making the decision to sell had taken him five years: years of soul-searching and guilty self-recrimination. It didn't help that he had no one—no one in the world—to discuss it with. His acquaintances—he couldn't call them friends—were few. He was closer to his lawyer than to anyone else, and what did that say about him? Nothing good.

Christos's bequest of the art collection, established by his father and increased with enthusiasm by himself, had come with a caveat: it was not to be sold or dispersed for a quarter of a century after his death.

'Why?' he'd asked the lawyer who'd explained it to him, when he was old enough to ask the question.

'He didn't say,' the man had replied. 'Presumably he simply wanted the collection to remain intact.'

'No.' Loukas had persisted. 'I mean why did he leave it to me? I was eight years old.'

The man had nodded, steepling his fingers. 'That is easier to answer. He felt responsible for the deaths of your parents. He took his duties as a godfather seriously. He wanted to provide for you. And,' he'd continued, 'of course, he did not expect to die so young.' He'd paused, glancing out of the window. 'Had he married and had a family of his own he might have changed his will. But that was not to be.'

'I was already provided for.' He'd been aware of the bitterness in his tone. 'My parents left me their shipping and property empire. I've never wanted for anything.'

Except a proper home, a family. Love. Whatever that was.

At the age of four he'd become a billionaire orphan, the subject of intense media interest and a target for kidnappers. Christos had curbed his jet-setting, playboy lifestyle to care for Loukas, limiting his trips away to European and American art fairs. He'd kept him on Alysos, where the only access was by sea or helicopter, employed a tutor and installed a security system. Four years later, it had ended in tragedy.

Alysos, where Loukas had been nurtured, protected and healed, now only symbolised loss and grief. It had taken him five years to make the decision to rid himself of the art collection that had burdened him since Christos's untimely death. To him, its existence was a painful reminder of the godfather he'd loved and of his own failure to protect him. He wanted the collection released from the vaults on Alysos and scattered across the world, like ashes, where it would no longer have the power to feed his guilt.

Once it had been catalogued and shipped, to

be auctioned, he'd never have to face his memories on Alysos again.

Choosing a reputable auction house to handle the sale had felt impossible. The thought of the publicity it would attract had almost made him change his mind. But if he avoided the big guns, the internationally famous names, he'd reasoned, perhaps the exposure could be kept more low-key and be better controlled.

Then, on a brief trip to London, he'd come across Marshalls. The entrance was discreet and it was the photograph in the window, of an ancient Greek vase, recently sold for an unprecedented sum, that had caught his attention. He'd returned to his Mayfair penthouse, around the corner, and looked them up.

Their response to his enquiry had been straightforward and professional, although the director had not been able to mask his excitement completely in his emails. Even so, making the final decision to sign the contract had taken several days—and nights.

But now, having their expert in this house, which had been shuttered for years, was more than difficult. It felt wrong. He bunched his fists, clenched his jaw and admitted to himself that he didn't know how he was going to get through it.

Loukas pushed himself upright and moved across the room to the desk. He pulled a bottle of single malt and a glass from the deep drawer, meant for files, and as he poured himself two fingers of the amber liquid, he cursed his shaking hand. Fingers wrapped around the weighty crystal tumbler, he turned to the window, swallowed a mouthful of the warming spirit and leaned his forehead against the cool glass.

The uneven, steep track disappeared into the gloom. Swirling the drink in his glass, Loukas tried to conjure up the image of the woman—Miss Shaw—who had climbed it earlier. Had he noticed that she seemed to favour her right leg, slightly, or had that just been his imagination? Then he remembered how she'd smoothed her hand over her right thigh. Had that been to dry a damp palm, or to soothe an ache?

Either way, he decided it was no concern of his. He reached out and released the cord of the blind, allowing the thick cream linen to tumble slowly over the window, closing out the darkness. Then he sat down in the leather chair, which had belonged to his godfather and which he himself had hardly used, since it had become his.

He'd known having a stranger here, examining the art and artefacts and cataloguing the collection, would be difficult. He'd thought he'd been prepared for that, but how did anyone prepare themselves for the complete unknown? And how would he feel when she wanted to discuss the removal of the items that had made this house what it was for a hundred years? Did he have a right to disturb things, separate items from each other that had been together for so long?

Those were all things he'd shelved somewhere in a compartment of his mind labelled 'deal with later'. Suddenly, 'later' had become 'now' and he wasn't sure he was ready.

Sophia Shaw unsettled him. He didn't understand it and he didn't like it. He couldn't rationalise that little flick of interest he'd felt when he saw her on the doorstep, or the faint sensation of…pleasure…he'd experienced at her unaffected delight at the view from the drawing room.

Anything that he couldn't rationalise made him uneasy.

He swallowed another slug of whisky and pulled a hand over his face. If he had a 'type' he didn't think she'd be it. He shook his head. No, not his hypothetical type at all. So whatever his reaction had meant, he could ignore it. Starting in the morning, he'd make sure that her task here was accomplished as fast as possible so she could get back to London and he to Athens, where he felt comfortable and…*safe*.

CHAPTER TWO

THE AEGEAN MORNING was exquisite, from the sun striking diamonds off the sapphire sea to the distant, misty shapes of neighbouring islands, and the immediate glory of the gardens spreading down the slopes around the villa. Sophia propped her elbows on the iron balustrade and took a deep breath, trying to clear her head and order her thoughts.

The tangy citrus scent of oranges hit her nostrils. The source of it was the tree that grew, gnarled and old, next to the terrace, its branches heavy with ripening fruit. She'd been shown to an elegant room the previous evening, decorated in restful shades of pale primrose and cream. French doors and shutters opened onto a stone terrace, where Anna had served her a simple meal. It was the perfect place to relax and unwind after a complicated journey, but although she'd had a long soak in the bath of the marble en suite, her sleep had been fractured.

Trying to equate the image she had formed in her mind of Loukas Ariti with the man who claimed to *be* him had kept her mind churning into the small hours. She felt as if a magician had played a trick on her that she couldn't understand. When she met him later this morning, which version of him would she find? The one in her head, or the very real, tall man with the tousled hair and obsidian eyes who had forgotten how to smile?

She pushed herself upright and turned to the breakfast tray that Anna had brought out to her. The sweet, dark coffee would help to kick-start her brain. She needed to be sharp for this meeting. Loukas Ariti might have signed on the dotted line, but he could afford to extricate himself from the contract if her professional performance wasn't sufficiently impressive. She was certain of that.

The door swung closed behind Sophia with a muted click and she felt as if she'd landed in a time capsule, or on the set of a play set half a century ago. A dark wooden desk, its surface protected by an old-fashioned blotter, dominated the room, and shelves jammed with old books lined the walls. The planked floor was partly covered by a worn Turkish rug. Sophia stood on the edge of it and clutched her laptop to her chest.

He—Loukas Ariti—stood at the window with his back to the room. As she studied his silhouette, that other image of him, which she had carried around in her head for weeks, dispersed like smoke into the warm air.

He looked taller, broader, than he had last evening. Black jeans hugged his slim hips, and a white linen shirt spanned the width of his shoulders.

Sophia's fingers curled more tightly around the edges of her laptop. She braced both knees and mentally adjusted her approach to this project. She had the feeling it was going to be unlike anything she'd ever undertaken. This man, with his dark eyes and air of solemnity, intrigued her. But her interest, and that of Marshalls, lay with his collection. She needed to remember that.

She took a breath.

'Mr Ariti—sir.' She tried to sound professional and assured, even though her usual routine looked as if it was about to be blown out of the water. 'It's...just after nine.'

Reading a person's movement was second nature to her and the tightly controlled shift of his body as he turned confirmed what she already suspected. He was tense as a bow string, from the severe line of his mouth to the biceps of his folded arms, which pushed against the fabric of his shirtsleeves, to his rigid thighs.

He nodded once, unfolded his arms and gestured towards the chair in front of the desk, before sitting down in the old leather one behind it. He shifted, as if the chair was uncomfortable. A frown drew his dark brows together as he leaned forward. His shirtsleeves were carelessly rolled

to the elbows, and he rested tanned forearms on
the desk.

'You wanted to discuss procedures. What do
you need to know?'

Evidently, he did not believe in wasting time on
pleasantries.

His voice was deeper than she remembered
from the previous evening, too, and huskier, and
his eyes...was it even possible to have eyes so
dark they appeared to be black, or was it because he was seated in front of the window with
the light behind him? His gaze was direct and
challenging and it was all she could do to hold it
with her own.

She expected to be given access to the collection, have the cataloguing system explained to
her, be told of any works that would be excluded
from the sale. All this should have been obvious
to the seller. On previous, similar projects she'd
walked into superbly organised private galleries,
or houses where everything had been prepared in
advance of her arrival, and she'd been able to get
on with the work almost immediately.

A handful of sales she'd arranged had been
different. They'd been occasions where the entire contents of a house or estate had been put
up for auction, down to the last silver teaspoon.
Those clearances had probably fetched a fraction
of the projected value of this one, if the rumours

of the contents of the Georgiou collection were to be believed.

This, she thought, putting her laptop on the desk and flipping it open, was going to be a different sort of challenge. Or *he* was.

'Well…perhaps we could start, Mr Ariti, by you telling me something about the collection? When was the last time you added to it, for instance? What is the estimated age of the oldest lot, and of the newest?' She tapped the keyboard, pulling up his file. 'That sort of information helps us to describe the sale and to set the tone. It allows us to attract collectors with a variety of specific interests.'

'I prefer Loukas, Miss Shaw.'

Had he heard anything she'd said, apart from his name? Sophia tucked her hair behind her ears and caught her bottom lip between her teeth. Her eyes met his over the top of the computer screen. His gaze roved over her face as if he was genuinely looking for something.

'Very well, Mr…Loukas. In that case, please call me Sophia.'

He nodded, then eased himself back in the chair, folded his arms again and tipped his head back so that he appeared to be studying the ceiling.

Sophia found herself distracted by the smooth olive skin of his throat, and the open top button of his shirt. He wore a white tee shirt under it.

And beneath that… She gripped her hands together in her lap.

'Nothing,' he said, just when she thought she was going to be forced to break the stretching silence, 'has been added to this collection for thirty years. Or, more specifically, since I inherited it. It was my godfather, Christos Georgiou, and his father before him, who were the collectors.'

In spite of her practice at retaining a professional demeanour, Sophia's eyes widened in surprise. This information was not common knowledge in the art world, although perhaps it gave substance to the rumour that no outsider had viewed the Georgiou collection for three decades, either.

'So you have been the guardian of this archive since you were…' She tried to calculate his age. 'You must have been a young boy—far too young for the burden of this kind of responsibility—when it landed on your shoulders.'

His eyes caught and held hers. A brief spark flickered in their dark depths, and then those shoulders lifted. 'I was eight. I can see you are trying to work it out.'

She smiled and nodded. 'Yes, I am, but it's complicated by the fact…'

He shook his head, and she sensed his leashed-in impatience, very close to the surface. 'The complications of how and why I inherited this…' he glanced down at the desktop and then his eyes came back to hers '…are irrelevant.'

'That wasn't what I was going to say. The complication is in my head, and it arises from the fact that you're about…two decades…younger than I imagined you to be. Do you realise how invisible you are?'

As soon as she'd asked the question, she realised how silly it was. For anyone to attain, and *maintain*, such a level of anonymity must have taken deliberate and prolonged determination. It was no accident.

The line of his mouth softened a little and his shoulders dropped a fraction. She couldn't have said he looked pleased, but he looked less unimpressed, and with a shock that delivered a kick to her stomach, sending it swooping downwards, she realised just how handsome he was, when he stopped frowning and relaxed, for a few seconds.

She dragged her attention from the slight curve of his lips, and from wondering what it would be like to be caught in the full beam of his smile, if it existed, and was immediately struck by the faint lines at the outer corners of his eyes. They might be laughter lines but were more likely the result of squinting in the bright Greek light. The hand that he raised to push through his hair was long-fingered and strong-looking. When he lowered it to clasp the other one on the desktop she noticed he wore no rings. A slim platinum watch circled one wrist.

His outward appearance betrayed no sign of

the immense wealth that she suspected lay all around her in this house. Despite her protestation, she found herself wondering at the circumstances of his inheritance. What kind of life must he have led, burdened by such responsibility from such a young age?

He tapped his knuckles on the unmarked white blotter. 'That pleases me… Sophia. My intention has always been to keep a low profile. You're telling me I have succeeded?'

'You must know you have but, yes, I am, which is why I need you to fill in some gaps for me. I—'

'Surely all you need to do is catalogue the works, and estimate their value? My personal life has no bearing on that.'

Sophia closed the lid of her laptop and sat back in her chair. If this was how he wanted to do things, she'd go along with him. She might need to save her arguments for later, and, while personal details of the vendor would give character and depth to the sale, it was perfectly possible for him to remain anonymous.

She crossed her right leg over her left and pushed her palm into her thigh. Her muscles ached from the energetic way she'd tackled the climb up the steps yesterday, and, as always, the ache in her right leg was deeper and more persistent than in her left. She saw him notice the movement and folded her hands together on top of her laptop, straightening her spine.

'If that is what you want, that is how we'll run the sale. It's just that buyers often like to know something about who they're buying from. If they feel a personal connection, however small, they're usually willing to pay more. But a twist of mystery could work to your advantage, too.'

He'd picked a pencil from the small glass jar on the desk—a Lalique vase, unless she was losing her touch—and was spinning it with an index finger on the desk in front of him, flicking it first one way, then the other.

'And,' she continued, when she received no response, 'we need to talk about advertising…'

'Advertising?' He stopped the twirling pencil and looked up, his eyes boring into hers.

'Yes. Promotion. We can't hold a sale, especially one of this size and importance, and not tell anyone about it. We want to attract the maximum number of high-net-worth individuals, museums and galleries with budgets to spend, governments who would like certain works returned to their own national collections, to make this the success it deserves to be.'

'No publicity. And no one may come here, especially not the press…'

Sophia took the time to inhale and exhale a couple of breaths. This was going to be difficult. Much more difficult than she'd thought. She'd have to take things slowly, which meant the whole operation would take longer to complete, but she was also going to have to convince him that promotion was unavoidable. She'd have to try to gain his trust, build it up gradually. Otherwise, she felt there was a real danger he would change his mind altogether.

To lose this deal would mean more than simply losing the fee. Marshalls would suffer from the loss of prestige, too. Other vendors would pass them over if they allowed the biggest sale in years to slip through their fingers. She knew she was good at her job, but could she persuade Loukas Ariti that she was good enough?

'We can certainly keep your face and possibly your name out of it,' she said, carefully considering the options. 'We could label it the…Christos Georgiou…if that was your godfather's name… collection.' She opened her laptop again. 'Since we finalised the contract I've worked on some ideas for promotion, although ultimately that will be in the hands of our advertising department. Once I've seen the artworks, I'll suggest one or two which might be used to illustrate our advertisements. Something which is well known, but which hasn't been seen in public for a long time, often proves irresistible to certain buyers. If you'd like to have a look…' She turned the computer to face him, but he stood up.

'I'll come round to your side. You'll need to guide me through it.'

He pulled up a second chair next to Sophia's

and leaned forward, resting his forearms on his thighs. Then he half rose and reached across the desk for a pair of rectangular, black-framed glasses. Sophia leaned forward to tap the keyboard.

As he stretched for his glasses, Loukas's shoulder brushed Sophia's forearm where it rested on the edge of the desk. For a beat of silence his body froze, shocked by the unexpected touch. She didn't seem to notice that the only barrier between his skin and hers was the white linen of his shirt. At the same time, he was enveloped in the light floral scent that surrounded her. He wanted to breathe in as deeply as possible, to store it in his memory, because it was the sweetest perfume he'd ever encountered. It felt so jarringly out of place in this sombre room that for a moment he felt disorientated, his mind dislocated.

Then he pressed his lips together and jerked his shoulder away, pulling his glasses towards him and putting them on. Luckily, sitting next to Sophia meant he didn't have to look at her. He didn't want to see any misunderstanding in her expression. It had been a fleeting error and he would make sure he didn't touch her again.

The chair scraped on the floor as he moved it slightly further away from her and tried to concentrate on the screen as she flicked through different promotional ideas, asking his opinion and making suggestions of her own. He closed his eyes briefly and pressed his fingers to his temples, finding it almost impossible to maintain his concentration this close to her.

It wasn't, he told himself, that he was especially aware of her. It was because he was so unused to engaging with strangers. He found being so close to someone else overwhelming. His sense of personal space was acute and his need for it had increased over the years. When you grew up with no one touching you, ever, even a cool handshake could be an ordeal.

When he opened his eyes he could feel she was watching him.

'Are you all right? I can send this to you to look at in your own time, if you prefer.' She clicked a button to exit the file. 'Or would you rather be shown the suggestions from the advertising department, when they've formulated their ideas?'

Loukas stood up abruptly, relieved to put a little distance between himself and this woman who had invaded his private space, even though it had been with his consent. He folded his glasses and slipped them into his shirt pocket.

'Yes.' He nodded. 'That would be best.' He watched as Sophia uncrossed her legs and rose to her feet. Intricate, plaited leather sandals displayed toenails painted in pearly pink polish that—he glanced at her hands—matched her fingernails. Her movements were expressive, even in the simple action of lifting the computer from the desk. He pulled his gaze away from her, alarmed at the way her presence distracted his thoughts. He needed to move this operation forward so she could get on with the work she'd come to do. He needed to wrap this up and get back to the life where he felt comfortable.

But while he was trying to concentrate on the practicalities that needed to be addressed, one thought dominated his mind: Sophia recognised that inheriting the art collection had been a burden. No one else had viewed it in that way. He'd only ever been envied, told how fortunate he was, when all it had been to him was a bitter reminder of how Christos's life had been cut short.

Yet Sophia had seen it, and acknowledged it, immediately. He wondered about her intuition, her empathy. Where had that come from?

He stepped around her, where she was busy sliding her laptop into its bag, and moved towards the door, anxious to escape the confines of the study. Her words had connected with him on an unfamiliar level and he needed to put a safe distance between them.

'If you'll follow me, I'll show you the office where you can work. It has direct access to the storage facility in the basement.'

Letting her—letting *anyone*—into the office and basement would be to cross a one-way bridge. She was about to get to see what countless collectors in the world of fine art had dreamed about for three decades. Once she stepped over the threshold, the absolute silence of those thirty years would be shattered. He held the study door open for her, then walked quickly away, before he could change his mind.

Sophia hoisted her bag onto her shoulder and followed Loukas. She had to walk quickly to keep up with his long strides and the bag banged against her hip. She ran her fingers over the skin of her forearm, where his shoulder had brushed against her, and wondered why his touch had felt so...unique. It had lasted only a moment and then he'd shifted sharply, as if he'd been burned. The tension she'd sensed coiling through his body had seemed to rob him of the ability to concentrate on the promotional ideas she'd been scrolling through on the screen in front of them. Either that, or the idea of publicity was so distasteful to him he refused to think about it at all.

He led her into a room furnished with a desk and banks of filing cabinets.

'This is the catalogue.' He made a sweeping gesture with an arm. 'It should be self-explanatory. Alphabetical, by name of artist. Painters along this wall.' He half turned. 'Sculptors along that one.' He shrugged. 'There're other disciplines, of course. Glassware, for instance, is in the filing cabinet behind the door.' He closed the door to reveal it. 'If any details of individual works are missing, that's because Christos didn't know them.' He walked over to a second door, in the further wall, pulling a key on a fob from his pocket. 'And through here are the stairs to the vaults, where everything is stored.'

Sophia stopped in the middle of the room.

'What about security? Surely the basement is protected by some sort of safety door. There must be an access code…'

Loukas turned, his hand on the door handle, and looked at her. Then he shook his head.

'No. That's unnecessary. The steps you climbed yesterday are the only way to the villa.' He strolled across to the window. 'The gardens you can see from your terrace end in sheer cliffs. The harbour and the neighbouring beach are the only places to bring in a boat and there is a security system, which is regularly updated.'

'But you, with your key, is all a would-be thief would have to get past…'

'I'm not here, most of the time. I live in Athens, but the cameras are monitored twenty-four-seven and the company has a hotline to the police on Skiathos. They'd be here by helicopter in minutes if they were alerted. Stephanos and Anna live here. They've been on the island since Christos's time.'

Sophia joined him at the window and looked out

over the terraced gardens, which fell away down the slope. She left a careful distance between them.

'I thought,' she said, slowly, 'that you lived here. A recluse.'

'"Recluse" is an exaggeration. "Private" is more accurate. I spend as little time here as possible.' A note of bitterness spiked the even tone of his voice.

'But it's so...beautiful. And private. Why wouldn't you prefer to live here?'

He turned his back on the pure light and distant, dancing waves.

'As I said, my personal life need not impact on this. You don't have to know the details of my living preferences to sell the collection. Once, I was happier here than anywhere else. But that changed.'

'I'm sorry,' Sophia said to his back. She pulled her laptop from the bag. 'Is that why you've decided to sell?'

He dipped his head, his hands thrust deep in the pockets of his jeans. His ebony hair curled at the collar of his shirt, but it didn't hide the tension she could see in the corded muscles of his neck. His shoulders lifted as his lungs expanded on a deep breath.

'You could say that.' He nodded. 'It's taken me a long time to reach this point. But...'

'How long?' Sophia pushed up the lid of the laptop and tapped the keyboard. 'We first heard that you might want to sell about two years ago.'

'I…' He shook his head again. 'You don't need to know any of this. It's irrelevant to the job you need to do. You'll find everything in order downstairs. The climate-control system keeps the humidity at optimum levels. Christos was fastidious about that, apparently. If you have any questions, make a note of them and I'll answer them at dinner. Now—'

'But, Mr Ariti—'

'Loukas.'

'*Loukas.* I need to access the digital catalogue on my computer. If you could give me the password before you go…'

'Nothing has changed here in thirty years, Sophia. There is no password. These filing cabinets should contain all you need.'

'Are you telling me this is the *only* catalogue? Surely it's been digitised? Backed up somewhere?'

He was at the door, looking as if he was in a hurry to leave.

'That's exactly what I'm telling you. Now, if you'll excuse me…'

Sophia stared at him, incredulous. She left the desk and followed him to the door.

'With a collection of this value, I'd call that grossly negligent.' She sucked in a deep breath, feeling her cheeks heat up.

'But you don't know its value. Your job is to calculate it. It may not be anything like as much as the art world apparently believes it to be.'

'It's rumoured that—'

'Rumours.' His voice snapped across the space between them, stopping her in mid-sentence. His eyes drilled into hers and she took a step back, shocked by the flash of pain that flared in their depths. 'Rumours have plagued me for most of my life.' His lids dropped, dark lashes shadowing his high cheekbones as his chest rose on an intake of breath. He pulled the door open. 'I'm not interested in rumours. I want you to do your job, establish the value and sell the collection. Every piece of it.' He turned away from her. 'If you will join me for dinner at seven,' he said, over his shoulder, 'I'll try to answer your questions then.'

Loukas strode towards his study but passed the door without missing a beat. The need to get out of the building intensified with every step he took. There wasn't a room or corner of it that didn't harbour memories and he was not in the frame of mind to confront them. Not now, when he'd decided to rid himself of all of them.

Once, he'd loved it here. To his boyhood self, the idea of living anywhere else, in spite of the cold fear he'd harboured deep in his soul, had been an impossibility.

Christos had been the perfect godfather. Loukas had idolised him, depended on him to keep him safe after the sudden, terrifying death of his parents. Christos had used gentle kindness to try to cure him of his horror of the sea, bit by bit, never pushing him too hard but employing constant encouragement. With infinite patience he'd taught him to swim in the pool and he, Loukas, had gained enough confidence to believe he might be able to attempt it in the sea, the following summer.

But how quickly everything could change.

He'd loved the British art collector and his wife and daughter who had visited on their motor yacht every summer. His first dim memory of them was of the summer after his parents had died. Christos had given a party for the girl's twenty-first birthday and joked that, at thirty, he was 'over the hill'. Loukas had wondered what that meant.

Many friends came to Alysos but Loukas had sensed from early on that these people were special. Christos had entertained them with an extra measure of generosity and taken immense care to ensure that their daughter was properly cared for and happy. They'd included Loukas in picnics and games. As his fear of the sea had diminished, they'd taken him to the beach where he'd played on the powder-soft sand while they swam. His memories were vague, but he knew Christos had visited them in London on his trips to art fairs.

Things were different, that last summer. At the age of eight he'd been old enough to be aware that Christos had been distracted, only interested in spending time with the girl. They'd gone for walks across the island without him, and taken the sailing dinghy out, for hours, returning looking flushed and guilty. He'd heard voices raised in anger. The normally tranquil air of Alysos had crackled with tension. And then there'd been the argument...

The door banged behind him as he left the house and took the rocky path up the craggy mountainside. When he reached the highest point on the island he searched for the boulder where he had liked to sit, as a boy, and from where the view stretched for as far as the eye could see in every direction.

He hadn't been here for thirty years, but nothing had changed.

He forced himself to look at the sea, to listen to the faint murmur of the waves as they washed ashore, diminishing to nothing on the sand, and the occasional rumble as a larger one crashed into the caves at the foot of the cliffs. The way the swells heaved themselves from the water, as if some huge creature were pushing them up from beneath, made him feel ill.

Then he made himself turn his eyes to the half-moon curve of white sand beyond the headland near the harbour. The perfect little cove was protected by cliffs at one end and a scatter of rocks at the other, giving privacy to anyone bathing, as well as anyone who might be watching.

Perhaps the memory burned into his brain would fade eventually. He pressed the heels of his hands into his eye sockets, knowing it was a futile hope. It visited him, in horrible detail, every day.

No one had visited Alysos since he'd been taken away to live with his tutor and his sister in Athens, but yesterday that had changed.

This woman—*Sophia*—moved like a dancer or an athlete, light on her feet, and quick, except for that hint of something uneven in her step that he almost saw but then thought he'd imagined. Her expressive hands almost spoke a language of their own.

When had he ever been distracted by a woman's hair, or the way she moved? Her presence unsettled him, and he wanted her gone, and this difficult time to be over, as quickly as possible. He'd finally reached the point where he could sell all this and consign it to history. He didn't want anything to interfere with his plans.

The last time visitors had been on the island his whole world had exploded in tragedy and when it had been reassembled its shape had been changed for ever.

This time, he would control the change. The new shape of his life would be in the form he chose.

CHAPTER THREE

SOPHIA LISTENED TO Loukas's footsteps recede along the hall and then she sat down at the desk. The screensaver on her laptop, a snowy scene of Clapham Common opposite her London flat, could not have been more different from the slice of view from the window in front of her.

Dazzling white walls, sprawling bougainvillea and vibrant hibiscus almost hurt her eyes with their intensity. The faded summer colours of England she'd left behind felt insipid by comparison.

Loukas's air of restless, wary energy made her uneasy. It felt as if he was constantly on the lookout for trouble, and needed to be on high alert to deal with it, whenever it happened. Whatever had happened on Alysos had scarred him. She knew how that felt, and a little ache of sympathy niggled at her. He was hurting. He'd been hurting for a long time.

And he seemed to be searching for something, studying her rather than simply looking at her. He might study the ceiling, or the surface of his desk, but then his eyes—those eyes that were almost black—would flick back to her face and rest there.

Could it really be possible that she was the first outsider to visit Alysos in three decades? If so, perhaps it was simply the presence of a stranger that made him uncomfortable.

She went over to the row of filing cabinets, pulling open the top drawer of the first one.

The files were neatly arranged in pockets, labelled with the names of artists. Some were eye-poppingly famous, others more obscure, and there were some she'd never come across before.

Trying to push the thoughts of Loukas to the back of her mind, Sophia extracted the first file and opened the door to the stairs that led down to the storage vaults.

She was going to get this done.

Dusk had softened the colours beyond the window when she finally shut down her computer. Her head swam with the images and statistics she'd uncovered. She'd methodically photographed each canvas, on her phone, and sent the images to her computer, where she'd compared them with a database of similar works that had been sold in the recent past. Then, based on her findings, she'd calculated what they might fetch in the current market.

Some of the paintings were rare, others better known when they'd last appeared on the open market. They were all in immaculate condition, which added to their value, and they were all meticulously catalogued in precise writing, in English and Greek.

From large abstract oils to tiny watercolour sketches, the collection had a broader reach and a more self-confident eclecticism than she'd ever encountered.

She knew something very important was unfolding before her eyes, that by some stroke of fortune she'd been given a once-in-a-lifetime opportunity to consign these works to auction.

It was hugely exciting.

Working carefully, she transcribed the details of each work onto her computer, creating a separate file for each artist and listing the works under type.

She made notes on her phone and a list of questions to put to Loukas, as he'd instructed her to do. Then she emailed her colleagues in London, attaching the files she'd completed. She'd leave it to them to decide which images they might use in the promotional campaign.

The choice was wide, and would grow wider, and she smiled as she imagined the discussions that would ensue about how to proceed.

No sooner had she clicked 'send' than her phone buzzed with a message from Sean.

Are you kidding me? Is this a joke?

No joke. It's altogether serious and quite over-whelming. And that's only A to B.

Can't believe we've landed this one. It's in your hands. Try not to screw it up.

His tone was tempered by a smiley face emoji, but Sophia felt the weight of real anxiety behind his words, and the responsibility that lay with her.

Screwing it up is not an option, even though the owner is...

She paused, put her phone down and looked out of the window at the fading view. The white walls had darkened to shades of indigo and the sea below gleamed, burnished by the rays of the sinking sun.

What could she say about Loukas? *Even though the owner is... Difficult? Likely to pull the plug at any moment? Jumpy?*

She caught her bottom lip between her teeth and picked up her phone again, her fingers hovering over the keys, then she deleted the message.

None of those words were the right ones. Although they might be true, she could not use them to describe Loukas. They didn't reflect the reality of what she'd seen of him.

But how could she say he was insightful, or damaged, or tense as a wire, without inciting an incredulous response from London? They'd think she'd had too much sun. Either that or too much ouzo.

Because after less than an hour in his company she felt a connection to him that somehow went deeper than she was yet prepared to admit, even to herself, and definitely not to anyone else.

She typed:

When have I ever screwed up? Or did that weird abstract with the unintelligible signature I couldn't identify turn out to be a long-lost Picasso?

She stretched, stiff from the long hours of sitting, picked up her laptop and removed the key from the lock of the inner door, realising that Loukas had not told her what to do with it. When she slipped it into her pocket, it felt freighted with significance and responsibility.

Her phone buzzed again.

Sadly not a Picasso. Perhaps you'll find one there?

Yeah, perhaps.

In this room, that possibility felt more likely than it ever had before.

* * *

Sophia crossed the terrace, skirting the pool with its hidden, underwater lights and stepping through the sliding doors into the vast drawing room. A faint streak of pink still coloured the western sky, but the sea glimmered like black glass, far below. In the distance the lights of other islands flickered and winked through the dark.

Soft lighting illuminated the room, pooling on deep-cushioned sofas and chairs and bringing the jewel colours of Persian rugs to glowing life. Along the back wall a series of portraits had been hung, each lit by an individual picture light. She strolled over to look at them, assuming they were family paintings and wondering if there would be one of Christos. It would be useful to have a picture of him to illustrate their advertising campaign and a painted portrait would have more impact than a photograph.

She wrapped her fingers around her phone in her pocket, ready to ask Loukas to point out Christos's portrait so she could snap a picture of it.

There were no framed photographs of family members on any of the surfaces in the room. The mantelpiece over the wide fireplace held a collection of Delft porcelain. If pictures had ever existed Loukas must have removed them to his home in Athens.

The direct gaze of a stately looking middle-aged woman caught Sophia's eye. She moved closer to the portrait, intrigued by the subject's patrician air, despite the hint of a smile on her lips. She'd been painted in a dress of royal-blue silk, with a plunging neckline trimmed in fine lace. Her hair was swept up into a complicated style, revealing a slender, elegant neck around which hung an intricate gold pendant, studded with seed pearls.

Sophia leaned in to look at the picture more closely.

'She was Christos's grandmother.'

The deep timbre of the unmistakeable voice behind her made her stomach drop and her shoulders stiffen. She turned her head so that she could see Loukas standing behind her.

One hand was thrust deep into the pocket of his black jeans, the other held a glass. As he raised it to his mouth, she caught the peaty scent of whisky. He swallowed and the smooth movement of his throat captured her attention. He shifted his weight on his feet and she wondered if his awareness of her felt as uncomfortable as hers did of him.

'Oh… I see.' She dragged her eyes away from the place at the base of his throat where the skin dipped into a hollow, back to the painting, hoping he wouldn't pick up on the irritating breathy huskiness in her voice.

'Would you like a drink before dinner? I believe the table is ready on the terrace.' He inclined his head towards the doors.

'Thank you. I'll have a glass of white wine. I was just looking…'

But Loukas had turned to lead the way towards the table. It had been set for two, near the balustrade at the edge of the terrace. The warm evening air brushed Sophia's skin as she stepped outside again. The breeze that had ruffled the water of the pool earlier had died and the surface lay smooth and undisturbed. While his back was turned, she tried to get her breath back to an acceptable rhythm. Hopefully her voice would behave, too.

He pulled out a chair for her.

Sophia smoothed her hands over her skirt and pulled her phone from her pocket, placing it on the table. Loukas glanced at it then lifted a bottle from the bucket of ice on a stand next to the table and poured wine into her glass. He raised his own, keeping his eyes on her.

'Thank you.' She sipped, grateful for the feeling of the cold, fresh tingle of the wine tracking down her throat. 'I—'

'How has your day been? Have you made any progress?' Loukas put his glass on the table and leaned on his forearms. He glanced at her phone again. 'I assume you have questions which you hope I'll answer.'

Sophia nodded, trying to concentrate on his

words rather than on the disturbing effect his voice had on her. It hit her in the chest, making her lungs squeeze and her heart beat to a faster rhythm. She dug her fingernails into her palms and returned his gaze, not altogether steadily. She thought about how she'd wanted to describe him to Sean, back in London, where he was stressing about whether or not she could pull off the assignment. Sean, and the discreet offices in Mayfair, seemed like a million miles away.

Since Loukas had closed the door and walked away from her this morning she felt changed in a subtle way. Realising exactly how important this collection was and how it might turn the world of fine art upside down had given her a sense of the privilege she was enjoying just by being a part of it. This was her job, her life. She was passionate about it and very good at it, but she knew this kind of assignment was unlikely ever to come her way again. The need to tread carefully, to get it right, was hugely important. How she handled this would define her career from now on.

That fleeting glimpse of the pain in Loukas's eyes, although he'd quickly masked it, had struck her deeply. Witnessing it had made her more cautious. There would have to be publicity. Without it there could be no sale. But she was determined to control it in a way that would cause him the minimum of discomfort. She wasn't about to tell Sean that he might be difficult, or touchy, and have him wading in and telling her how to manage the project. She'd keep the information she sent back to London strictly factual and impersonal. Since the collection would be referred to as Christos's, if she got her way, Loukas could remain anonymous.

The relationships she established with clients were special and each one was unique. She had to allow for their wants and needs, understanding that sometimes parting with treasured possessions was deeply painful for them. But she didn't think the sale of this collection was the cause of Loukas's reserve or discomfort. He'd decided to sell a collection to which he hadn't added in thirty years. That alone told her his interest in it was academic rather than personal.

The reason for what she'd seen in his dark eyes must go much deeper than that and it had engendered an irrational determination in her to protect him.

Anna brought flatbread with olive oil to dip it in and bowls of aromatic chilled soup to the table. Sophia watched as Loukas tore the bread, his long fingers delicate and strong. She picked up her spoon.

'So,' he said, 'what did you think of Christos's grandmother? You seemed to find her rather engaging.'

Sophia nodded, pleased to begin the conversation on a neutral subject.

'I did. Is it a good likeness, do you think? I presume you never knew her?' She crumbled a piece of bread on her plate, then sipped a spoonful of the soup.

'Never. I only knew Christos, but the pictures were all painted by reputable portrait artists, so I think it's probably a good likeness, yes.'

She dipped a piece of bread into the oil. 'Mmm. This is delicious.'

'The oil is made from olives grown on Alysos. Some of the trees are centuries old.'

She glanced towards the drawing room, where the row of portraits hung in their own pools of light. 'I was attracted by the pendant she's wearing. It's in the shape of a heart, decorated with pearls. I think it's a locket.'

Anna removed the empty soup bowls and replaced them with plates of fragrant rice and spicy lamb skewers.

Loukas thanked her in Greek, and Sophia nodded her appreciation.

'Yes,' he said, eventually. 'You're right. It's a locket. It was a family piece, but it's been lost, somehow.'

'What a pity.' Sophia swallowed a mouthful of wine. 'It's very pretty.'

The food was delicious, and Sophia found herself relaxing, beginning to enjoy Loukas's company. The still night air, laden with the scent of herbs and lavender, was the perfect temperature for eating outdoors and the distant sound of the pull and push of the sea was calming. But when she asked him the questions she'd accumulated and he answered the ones he could his manner was guarded.

As they finished the meal with cheese and fruit, he asked her a question of his own.

'How long,' he said, 'do you think you'll be here?'

His eyes were on hers, making it difficult for her to concentrate.

'I… At the moment I'm not sure. It depends…'

'Surely,' he said softly, 'you can give me an estimate? Days? Weeks? *Longer?*'

'More than days…weeks, perhaps…'

'I'm not going to hold you to whatever you say, Sophia. I'm simply interested. The collection has lain here for thirty years. A few weeks more is hardly going to make much difference.'

'Weeks, then. About two, I think. But you've said, more than once, that I must get the work done as quickly as possible. And there'll still be transportation to be arranged. Specialist packers. Insurance…'

He held up a hand. 'Stop. I don't need to know any of that. I'll leave Anna and Stephanos to deal with those details.'

'I promise to finish as quickly as possible. But I can't predict that it will all be easy. There may be some works which need further research, which

I might not be able to do here. Second opinions might be necessary…'

'Yes. I understand that. I simply thought you'd be anxious to get back to your life in London, your family…'

Family. How would it feel to have one of those?

She thought about the Kensington house she'd inherited from her grandparents, filled with furniture, silver, and porcelain, the walls crowded with paintings. It had never felt like a home. It wasn't somewhere she could take friends from school, even if she'd been allowed to. What friends would want to go to tea in a museum, where they'd be warned not to touch anything?

In her imagination she'd designed the perfect home. It had a garden with an old apple tree and a swing, and the house was warm and welcoming, with a cosy kitchen and a sitting room with squashy sofas and a fireplace. She'd completed the house by adding a husband and two children, and a dog.

Once, she'd thought her dream was within reach, but now it felt like an impossibility.

Her flat in Clapham was small but she'd fitted in a squashy sofa.

One day, she'd sell her grandparents' house and its contents. One day, when she'd managed to distance herself from it. Because memories, and hope, still tied her to it.

Memories, gleaned from things her grandparents had let slip, when they'd thought she couldn't hear them, of the mother she had never known. The things they *had* said to her had been hurtful and frightening. Her mother had suffered from a heart condition. She'd been told she must never have children, but then, they'd said, fixing her with accusing stares, she'd had *her*. She'd survived long enough to say she wished her to be named Sophia, but then her damaged heart had stopped beating.

They never actually said the words, but they'd always hung in the air. *You killed your mother, our only daughter.* She never needed to ask them who they would have preferred to live.

Once, when she was thirteen, she'd dared to ask about her father. It had taken her days to screw up the courage to do it. A girl at school had questioned her about him, and she'd hoped to be able to say he was someone glamorous and famous, but her grandparents had simply glared at her and told her he was dead and she must never speak of him again. What was worse, on her birth certificate he was entered as 'unknown'.

Sophia dragged her thoughts back to the present and found Loukas's steady gaze fixed on her face. He'd said something about family.

'Family?' she said, shaking her head. 'No, I don't have a family. I was raised by my grandparents.'

He looked unconvinced. 'But surely there must be someone?'

'No.' She thought it must sound strange. Loukas probably came from a large and loving Greek family, with a clutch of relatives, from grandparents to baby nephews and nieces, who gathered together for Christmases and birthdays and always looked out for each other. 'No,' she repeated. 'My mother was their only child and my father died before I was born. I don't know anything about him.'

Loukas picked up a teaspoon and studied it, running his fingers over the smooth silver, then he looked across at her again.

'So you won't be in a hurry to get back.'

'If you're concerned,' she answered carefully, 'that I might stretch the assignment out for longer than necessary, you don't need to be.' She took a sip of water and replaced the glass on the table. 'Marshalls has an impeccable reputation for professionalism.'

Loukas put the spoon down. He nodded. 'I apologise. I wasn't calling your integrity into question.'

Sophia smiled. 'I can understand why you might think I'd like to stay as long as possible. I've wanted to explore the Aegean islands for a long time and the area is even more beautiful than I expected. And apart from that, I feel as if I'm—*absorbing* ancient history, myths and legends with every breath.'

His eyes held surprise and interest. 'You haven't been to Greece before?'

'I attended a conference in Athens a couple of years ago, but out here it feels like a different world, one in which time has stood still in many ways. Ancient ruins are simply a part of the landscape, and the faces of the people...' She dropped her eyes, suddenly self-conscious.

'What about them?'

'Some of them...even you...' she glanced up at him '...remind me of descriptions from *The Odyssey*.' She picked up the linen napkin from her lap and folded it over, pressing her thumb along the crease. 'I'm sorry. I didn't mean to sound so personal.'

'Not at all. I'm intrigued by your observations.'

A waft of cool air, laden with the tang of the sea, ruffled the surface of the pool and whispered through the bougainvillea above them. Loukas glanced over his shoulder towards the drawing room.

'Are you cold? Shall we move indoors?'

He stood. Then he waited behind her while she rose from her chair.

The furniture in the spacious room was arranged in groups, lamps casting intimate pools of light over sofas and chairs.

'Sit down, Sophia. Would you like a liqueur? A brandy? Something local?'

'No, thank you.' Sophia chose the corner of a

deep sofa. 'I mustn't stay much longer. I need to check my emails.'

Loukas moved to a drinks cabinet and poured a measure of brandy. Cradling the balloon glass, he sat in an armchair opposite her. 'Emails? I thought you'd finished work for the day.'

She lifted her shoulders. 'I like to be up to date at the end of each day. It means everything runs more smoothly and quickly. I'm hoping to have time to spend a couple of days at the end of the assignment exploring some of the other islands, so working hard is in my interests as well as yours.'

Loukas swirled the deep amber liquid in the glass. 'Do you know where you'd like to go?'

'That will depend on how much time I have and how Sean is feeling. This is an important job and he's anxious to have me back on the team in London.'

He sipped the brandy and placed the glass on the table between them. 'Where did you spend your last holiday?'

'Rome and Florence. I needed to revisit some of the museums.'

'That sounds like work. Do you ever go to the beach and lie under an umbrella and read a book?'

Sophia bit her lip. Lying on a beach wasn't something she could imagine doing again. She shook her head. 'No. I like to be busy, experiencing new things. I read in the evenings.'

'It sounds as though your grandparents took you on educational holidays and you've never kicked the habit.'

'Actually…' She stopped. The conversation was heading towards uncomfortable territory.

'Actually what?'

'They said their travelling days were over. We didn't go on holidays.'

She started to get up but Loukas leaned forward and rested his elbows on his knees.

'Did you like living with your grandparents?' he asked.

Sophia considered his question for a moment, surprised by his interest. 'It wasn't a question of liking it. It…was all I knew. I had everything I needed.' *Except loving kindness.* 'But the house was…*is*…like a museum. Not homely.'

'Do your grandparents still live there?'

'No. They died within months of each other, three years ago. I'll sell it, some time.' She dropped her eyes to where her hands were gripped together in front of her, white knuckles gleaming under the skin. 'My mother died when I was born, but she grew up in the house and I feel a…connection…to her in it. When I get past that, I'll be ready to sell.'

'Is that what you want?'

Sophia thought about her answer. Her connection to the house had always felt like a barrier. If she could shed the feelings and emotions that tied her to it, she thought she'd find it easier to make a life separate from her past.

'Yes. I feel held back by it.' She saw his eyes drop to her hands.

'Your memories of your grandparents must be bound up with the house, too.'

'Not good memories. Although they never said the words, the implication was always that I was responsible for my mother's death. Which is true. I was.'

Loukas's gaze narrowed.

'Your mother wouldn't have wanted you to feel that way.'

Wouldn't she?

'I have no idea what she would have wanted. I hoped to find out something about her, going through my grandparent's papers, but there was almost nothing. I've never even seen a picture of her.'

'And you still live in this house? On your own?'

'No, I moved out when I was a student. Now I live in a flat in Clapham, opposite the common. I check on the house, of course. I revisit all the things that fascinated me as a child—the pictures, especially. It wasn't all negative. That environment nurtured my love of art and antiques. It's why I do what I do today.'

When she'd been planning for the future she imagined, she'd been happy, but that had changed.

Her future looked very different now. She didn't tell him that, or about her mother's room, which had been locked all her life. She still hadn't had the courage to open the door, even though her grandparents had been dead for three years.

She'd left out much more than she'd told, but suddenly she wondered why she'd told him anything at all. The story of her childhood was not something she normally shared with anybody, especially not a man she'd known for little over twenty-four hours and who happened to be an important client. The soft lighting, the comfortable furniture, the quiet, all contributed to an ambience of intimacy that had seduced her into feeling as if they were in a bubble of safety and trust.

She was reluctant to burst it but she knew she had to re-establish the boundary between them Those feelings were treacherous. You were only ever as safe as the moment allowed you to be, and the best person to trust was yourself.

But Loukas had a way of asking questions that allowed no wriggle room. He was direct and sincere and he seemed to be genuinely interested in her responses and she hadn't considered refusing to answer him. Probably nobody ever did.

'It must be easier for you,' she said, trying to shift the conversation from herself to him, 'not having a personal connection to the collection you're sending to auction.'

'Not to the collection, no. But to Christos…my

connection to him…that's why this feels so difficult. Sometimes I think it's a betrayal.'

His jaw tightened and his brows drew together. She had a sudden need, completely at odds with her attempt to put distance between them, to stretch out a hand to him, to tell him it was a brave decision. She shook her head, trying to dispel the inappropriate thought. He dragged a hand over his jaw and closed his eyes.

'Sometimes,' she said, 'it's easier to leave things as they are. It must have taken courage to decide to sell the collection, not because you care about it, but because afterwards nothing will ever be the same again. I feel privileged to have this opportunity to see Alysos before it changes.' She looked round. 'It's so beautiful. And peaceful.'

His eyes, when he opened them, were bleak. His voice was roughened. 'It hasn't always been peaceful.'

His words seemed to come from a dark well of sadness. Sophia watched him swallow a mouthful of brandy, the muscles of his throat tense. She wondered what could have happened to shatter the tranquillity of this isolated island to cause him such anguish.

She longed to ask, but the question felt much too personal and his gaze seemed to have turned inwards, as if he was reliving some traumatic event of the past. Then his eyes returned to her face and with it his attention. A muscle ticced in his jaw.

'This,' he said, 'is where you ask me what happened.'

Sophia shook her head. 'No,' she said, 'I don't think so. You'll find I'm a sympathetic listener if you want to tell me, but it doesn't look as if you do.'

It was a long time before he spoke again. Then he pushed a hand through his already messy hair and straightened up. 'No.' His tone was resolute. 'You're right. Talking wouldn't change things. Nothing can change the past.'

'That is true, but sharing things can help us to perceive them in a different way, see them from someone else's point of view.'

'You sound as if you speak from experience.'

'Yes, I do. Apart from the circumstances of my upbringing, there've been difficulties I've had to overcome in my life. If I'd locked them away and never spoken about them, I would never have moved on, in another direction. I wouldn't have been here, for instance. And I'm very grateful that I am.'

He nodded. 'Deciding to sell hasn't been easy but I will go through with it.' He glanced towards the back of the room where the row of portraits hung. 'I wish I knew what Christos really wanted me to do, but in the absence of that information I have to go with what I want.'

Sophia followed his gaze, pleased that the conversation had shifted back to the subject of the art collection. 'Is there a portrait of Christos? I'd like to take a photo of it, if there is. We can use his image in the promotional material, if that's what you'd prefer.'

Loukas rose in a smooth movement and motioned for Sophia to follow him across the room to the row of portraits.

'This is the one of Christos. It was painted shortly before he died.' He swallowed. 'He was four years younger than I am now.'

Christos had been painted on the terrace with the backdrop of the sea and distant islands. Fitting, thought Sophia, for a man with his swashbuckling, piratical air. From his thick, dark hair, to his mischief-seeking eyes and amused, sardonic smile, he exuded a magnetic charm.

'May I?' She raised her phone, glancing towards Loukas for permission.

He nodded, but she hesitated, stopped in her tracks by the look of pain mixed with love on his face. He turned and moved into the shadows, away from the lit portraits.

'Please. Go ahead.' There was strain in his voice, which she could tell he was struggling to master.

'You loved him very much.'

'Yes. I did.'

Sophia took the picture and slipped her phone

back into her pocket. She could check it later and take another one tomorrow, if necessary, but she suddenly wanted to escape the charged atmosphere in the room. She followed Loukas and stopped next to him at the glass doors.

The pain had been wiped from his face and replaced with his usual, sombre expression. He stood with his arms folded. She stepped past him, and turned.

'Thank you for dinner,' she said, backing away from him. 'I hope you will sleep well.'

CHAPTER FOUR

LOUKAS PACED THE floor of the study. He knew sleep would be impossible. He was on edge and irritable, stress making him feel that he might explode if he didn't do something to relieve the pressure of the thoughts in his head.

He'd planned to leave the Marshalls' representative here, under the care of Stephanos and Anna, and return to the seclusion of his penthouse in Athens. The shipping and property empire he'd inherited on the death of his parents frequently required his presence, either in one of the international offices or at his home, usually to sign a pile of documents.

When he'd been taken away from Alysos, no regular school could be found that was prepared to tolerate the constant presence of a bodyguard for an eight-year-old child, but his wealth had put him at a high risk of kidnap. The solution had been found in the form of his tutor's sister who had agreed to have them both living with her. But he'd turned into a rebellious teenager and eventually been sent to a school in Switzerland, where sport had been regarded as just as important as academic study. He'd become a competitor on the winter slopes and the summer tennis courts and he'd learned to curb his competitive nature and his temper.

He'd studied finance at university in Britain and then begun to learn the ropes of the business his parents had bequeathed him. Living a modest life under an assumed name, he'd avoided the attentions of the tabloid press and any bounty hunters who might have taken an interest in him and worked across the world on high-profile projects. His business empire had been efficiently run by an expert team while he was growing up and when, in his thirties, he'd felt qualified to do so, he'd slipped into his inherited role as the head of the company.

But the villa on Alysos and the priceless collection stored in its vaults had plagued him, long before the twenty-five-year date had loomed. He hated the idea of it. Both the place and its contents were responsible for the worst, most terrifying events of his life.

Until that fateful day, his life on the island had been charmed. Christos had made sure of that. He'd taken on a terrified, traumatised child, out of a sense of duty to his oldest friend, and helped him to heal. He'd even helped him to overcome his terror of water, but not for long.

In this state of mind, he knew the flashbacks lurked just on the edge of his brain, waiting to torment him. And if he tried to sleep, the nightmare would visit him and he'd wake, sweating, hearing the scream that still haunted him after all these years.

He should send Sophia back to London and request someone else in her place. She made him feel unsafe, as if she had the power to unlock the door behind which he kept his emotions, and if that happened, he didn't know what would become of him. He'd fall apart, definitely. But after that? How would he ever get himself back together?

Sending her back to London would incur the wrath of her boss. She might lose her job or her position in the hierarchy of the company. This assignment was huge and important. The commission Marshalls would earn from it was large and the prestige it would bring them was of incalculable value. Sophia's career would be given a massive boost.

He could not risk taking that away from her, simply because she tapped into emotions he'd rather not acknowledge.

Her kindness made him want to talk, to share things with her that he never shared with anyone.

She made him want to change his plan to return to Athens. Although he hated being here, being ambushed by memories at every turn, for the first time, ever, since he'd been taken away, he wanted to be here and experience her unexpected warmth and open-heartedness.

Her blue, blue eyes, sparkling in the candle-light at dinner, her wide smile, and her golden hair, brushing the delicate skin of her collarbones, simply entranced him.

Just like the blonde girl who had entranced Christos.

He pressed his fingers into his temples and groaned, shaking his head.

This was a massively unfortunate coincidence. Sophia's arrival had been planned. Her visit had not come out of the blue, like some portent of doom. To compare it with what had happened thirty years ago was crazy. He needed to strengthen his grip on reality.

For the second time that day, he felt as if his surroundings were crowding in on him, and he had to get out. He left the study, retracing his steps towards the drawing room and then stepping through the doors onto the terrace.

Sophia threw off the fine linen sheet and sat on the edge of the bed, feeling the cool marble tiles of the floor beneath her feet. She sighed, and pressed her fingers to her temples, massaging them in slow circles, trying to bring her thoughts under control.

Her mind was on a treadmill that she couldn't turn off.

Why had she shared those details of her life with Loukas Ariti? What had possessed her to do it? She never talked about her past. The facts were painful, some of them were humiliating, and no one needed to know them.

Just as Loukas had insisted that details of his personal life were not pertinent to the job she'd come to do, neither were hers. He didn't need to know anything about her, apart from the fact that she was employed by Marshalls and had been entrusted with this task.

She pushed herself off the bed and walked to the en suite bathroom, flicking on the light above the mirror.

Her reflection did nothing to soothe her agitation. Her hair was tousled from tossing backwards and forwards on the pillows, her skin pale. Circles under her eyes made them look faintly bruised. She splashed cold water on her face, turned off the light and then made her way to the French doors and stepped out onto the terrace.

A silver segment of the moon hung low in the sky, in its own pale halo of light. The stars, cast across the vast universe, winked like diamonds. Far below, she could hear the shushing sound of the sea on the sand.

She longed for a swim. It would calm her mind, reset her mood. Swimming had long been her favourite exercise and she needed it now, but she knew it would be foolish to try to negotiate the rocky path down to the harbour in the dark.

And then she remembered the pool, just a few steps from the door of her suite.

She opened a drawer and contemplated her swimwear. There was a choice between the wet-suit, which covered her arms to the elbows and her thighs to the knees, or a bikini. It was pitch dark and after midnight. Nobody was going to see her. She pulled the bikini out of the drawer and wriggled into it.

The surface of the pool was like a dark mirror to the night sky. The water was warm and silky against her skin as she slipped under the surface and swam a few strokes, emerging with a quiet splash at the infinity edge and resting her chin on her folded arms. Then she pushed off and began to swim laps, slicing through the water with efficient, economical strokes.

The exercise stretched her muscles, and she felt her right thigh begin to soften and relax as she swam. She loved the way the water supported her but also resisted her as she pushed against its weight. It was what had made swimming her favourite therapy, after the accident and subsequent surgery. It had strengthened her thigh muscles, wasted from months of being immobilised in a cast, and helped to tone the rest of her. The repetitive rhythm of the strokes acted like a meditation on her mind, helping her to keep things in perspective and her life on track.

Her right leg would always tire more quickly than her left, and she was trying to be less self-conscious about the scar. She counted herself lucky to be alive. A gifted and committed surgeon had saved her leg, against all odds, and she owed it to the hospital team, who had worked so hard for her, to make a success of her recovery.

At last, breathing fast, she slowed her stroke and glided to the edge. She twisted, pulled herself out of the water and sat on the side, pulling her knees up to her chin. The underwater lights cast wavering shadows on the bottom of the pool, but then a different shadow, solid and dark, fell across the marble terrace next to her and she looked up into the eyes of Loukas.

'Oh…you startled me.' She began to scramble to her feet. 'I…couldn't sleep and I needed some exercise. I've been working all day, sitting at the desk…'

He wore the same jeans and shirt, but his feet were bare, and he held a large towel out towards her.

'I came out for some fresh air. I don't sleep well, either. The swimming towels are in that chest.' He glanced towards a white wooden chest. 'Next time you need one.'

'Thank you. I'm sorry if I disturbed you. I'll go in now.' Sophia grabbed the towel and quickly wrapped it around her body, tucking it under her armpits. Her legs shook slightly from the exercise and, to her horror, as she turned her right one gave way. She lurched, hoping she'd fall into the pool and not onto the marble tiles, but she didn't fall at all.

Loukas's strong hands caught her and as he pulled her upright she collided with the hard muscles of his chest.

'I'm sorry,' Sophia said again. 'My leg gave way. I must have swum for longer than I realised. It gets tired…' Her forehead was pressed against his collarbone. 'I'm making your shirt all wet.'

'My shirt will dry.' She felt the words rumble through his chest. 'Why does your leg get tired?'

'Oh, it's nothing. Nothing you need to know, anyway.'

Sophia tested the weight on her right leg. 'I think I'll be all right now. Thank you for catching me.'

'Are you sure you're not going to fall over?'

She felt his hands slide off her shoulders and he stepped back, watching her closely.

'Yes, I'm sure.' But then she began to shiver. Wildly, Sophia thought that she'd only started shivering when he'd pulled away from her, breaking the contact between them. Standing pressed against his hard body she'd been perfectly warm and she'd wanted to stay there And she'd felt something else, too. She tried to define what it was. She'd felt safe, as if she belonged, in some unique, totally unexpected way.

'You're cold. You should go in and have a hot shower.'

But the only place she belonged was in her flat in Clapham, or in her office at Marshalls. That was where she fitted, where she felt accepted. Where nobody saw her scar and nobody knew that she had been the reason her mother had died.

The thoughts tumbling through her head made her shiver more. She clenched her jaw to stop her teeth from chattering. Any good the swim had done was swiftly unravelling.

'Y-yes.' She nodded, the chill intensifying as a cool breeze blew across her skin. 'I'll go in for a shower. G-goodnight.'

Her first step was hesitant, and Loukas closed the gap between them.

'Let me help you.'

'No. I'm really okay...'

But she stood still, afraid to move in case she stumbled. Her damaged leg felt unreliable and her shivering intensified, fuelled by the worry of falling. She tried to centre herself and focus. Inhaling the breath she needed was hampered by the chattering of her teeth.

'May I?' Loukas raised an arm, and she nodded. He put it loosely around her shoulders, guiding her towards the door to her suite.

She felt the warmth of his hand on her upper

arm. Heat spread through her body, but she still shivered. His arm tightened about her as he pushed the door open with his free hand, pressing a switch so that the room was bathed in soft light. At the bathroom door she turned to thank him.

Only the towel separated her body, in her wet bikini, from the solid strength of his broad chest. Just for a moment she felt that delicious sense of *belonging* again. She clenched her fists more tightly.

Her eyes were level with his undone top buttons and her mouth was scarcely an inch from his chest. Dropping her gaze, she could see the damp imprint her wet bikini had made on the white linen fabric of his shirt.

She tipped up her chin. A brief flame flared in the dark depths of his eyes, and she knew their thoughts had collided. She wanted to stand on tiptoe and brush her mouth across his lips, feel the rasp of his jaw against her smooth cheek, and she was certain he wanted that, too.

An electric charge seemed to arc between them as he held her gaze, and a dangerously unstable chemistry threatened to ignite.

But the idea of spontaneous intimacy frightened her. She needed to prepare herself to be seen in this sort of situation. What if Loukas was shocked by the ridged scarring of her disfigured thigh? What if he turned his head away, sickened by the sight?

It had happened before and she remembered with vivid clarity how she'd shrivelled inside.

Loukas took a step back, smoothing his hands over her shoulders before thrusting them into his pockets. Sophia leaned against the doorframe for security.

'I'll…be fine now. Thank you.'

'I think I need to ask you not to go swimming alone.' There was a rough edge to his voice. 'What if I hadn't been there to catch you? You might have fallen into the pool and banged your head. You might…' He twisted his head away and looked towards the window. 'So, if you don't mind…'

'But I'm a strong swimmer. I love swimming. It's my favourite exercise. It's what helped my leg to heal, and—'

'You still haven't told me about your leg, but, even if you didn't have an injury, I'd rather you only swam with someone else present. It's sensible practice.'

'Do you mean with you?'

She saw his shoulders tense and rise before he seemed to make a conscious effort to relax them. He shook his head.

'Not with me. I don't swim.'

'You don't swim?' Sophia thought she must have misheard him. 'How can you live on a Greek island in the Aegean and *not* swim? Do you mean you *can't* swim?'

'No. I mean I *don't* swim. I…choose not to.'

Sophia frowned, studying him for clues. It didn't seem as if he was going to enlighten her.

'Why?' She raised a hand to push her wet hair off her forehead. 'There must be a very good reason not to swim, in this environment.'

'Not one that I wish to share.' He looked down at his feet. 'Remember, you don't need to know the details of my life in order to do your job. And remember that I don't live here. I live in Athens.'

Sophia watched him walk to the door. Then he turned. 'Next time you want to go swimming, please let me or Anna know.'

'Even if it's the middle of the night?'

There was a beat of silence. His eyes clung to hers and she saw his jaw tighten.

'Especially if it's the middle of the night.'

'But if you don't swim you wouldn't be able to rescue me, anyway.'

'Possibly not.' The door closed behind him.

Sophia stood under the powerful jet of hot water for a long time, until her teeth had stopped chattering and she felt warmed through.

She tried to scrub away the feeling of his hand on hers, the memory of the way their eyes had clashed, the peril of that almost-kiss.

She ran her fingers over her lips. The unforgiving line of his mouth had softened as they'd stared at each other, inches from doing something totally insane. His eyes had warmed. He'd wanted to kiss her as much as she'd wanted to kiss him.

But they'd stopped it. Still buzzing with desire, she couldn't decide if that had been the best decision she'd ever made, or the worst.

Loukas leaned against the balustrade looking out to sea but only seeing Sophia's pale face turned up towards him, with her eyes deepened to midnight blue in the dark and her full, kissable lips slightly parted.

He rubbed his fingers over his eyes. When last had he wanted to kiss a woman with such fierce desire that he had almost given in to it? He couldn't remember, and the force of these feelings almost floored him.

With his legendary wealth and dark good looks, any number of women were available to him. Polished, elegant, sophisticated, they wore high heels and wrap-around sheath dresses and their hair in stiff, complicated styles. He dated some of them. Some he slept with. But he never stayed a whole night or entertained any of them in his own apartment.

He'd grown up wanting for nothing, except a loving environment. He had no experience of love or emotional intimacy, and he didn't do relationships. He wouldn't know how. Any woman he dated had to understand that from the beginning.

No one would want to discover that behind

the billionaire's smooth façade was the eight-year-old boy who was afraid of water. He had seen the depths of despair and misery that unrestrained passion and unleashed anger could lead to, in the blink of an eye. He'd never risk exposing himself to them again.

He couldn't recall the last woman he'd dated. The mental turmoil that he'd endured, reaching the decision to sell Christos's art collection, had taken up all his energy. He'd had none left for small talk, or pillow talk, and now the only face he could see in his imagination was Sophia's.

Was his recent lack of female company the reason he found her so…beguiling? He didn't believe it was. She was totally unlike any of the women he'd known. Fresh and natural, radiating a fierce intelligence, she'd disturbed him from the moment she arrived, in her pretty cotton dress and plaited sandals. He knew he should leave her here, as he'd planned, to complete the cataloguing of the collection and to organise it to be shipped to London for auction. But he knew now he wouldn't be able to do that.

She'd stirred something in him that he couldn't yet identify but he wouldn't rest until he could. He wanted to engage with her, find out more about her, watch her as she worked through the pictures and artefacts. Her movements, quick and light, fascinated him. When he'd come across her in the pool, he'd stood for a moment, watching her perfect stroke as she'd completed her last lap. The economical way she'd sliced through the water with barely a splash, the soft sound of her steady breathing, had mesmerised him. In that moment, he'd felt calm and at peace for the first time in many months.

He'd met her a little over twenty-four hours ago. They'd engaged in the most formal of conversations, about the job she had to do here.

Except, he thought, for this evening over dinner, when she'd told him a little about her upbringing. The idea of Sophia, with her open demeanour and warm personality, growing up in what sounded like a loveless, cold environment angered him. What grandparents would treat their only living relative in such an unfeeling, callous way?

He supposed they thought the inheritance they were leaving her would be compensation for her lonely childhood and adolescence. He knew only too well how wrong that assumption was. Nothing—*nothing*—could compensate for an upbringing devoid of affection or kindness.

And she'd obviously suffered a traumatic injury at some point. He remembered watching her determined climb up the path yesterday. Now he knew her leg had probably been painful and tired, but she hadn't mentioned it or complained.

As she'd scrambled to her feet at the side of the pool, he'd glimpsed a long scar on the inside of her right thigh. Perhaps she'd had a shattered femur, and surgery to repair it. Whatever it was, he was glad he'd stopped her from swimming alone. The injury obviously bothered her, possibly when she least expected it. He needed to protect her from the dangers of water.

From where he stood, he could see along the side of the villa, to the place where the light from Sophia's French window fell in pale stripes through the shutters. He watched until it went out and he assumed she was safely in bed, hopefully asleep.

Then he went back into the drawing room and forced himself to stand before the portrait of Christos for a minute, remembering his wicked sense of humour and his sardonic smile. He crushed the doubts that rose in his mind. It was no use beating himself up about whether Christos would have cared about the break-up of his collection of art. It was his to do with as he pleased. He had to at least try to move on. He turned his back on the portrait, poured himself a whisky and took it out onto the terrace.

He skirted the edge of the pool carefully and stretched out on one of the steamer chairs, balancing the glass on his chest and tilting his face up to look at the stars. If he fell asleep, which he doubted, he hoped he would dream of the feel of a slight, strong woman in his arms and not of a violent argument and a scream, or the weight of water.

CHAPTER FIVE

IT HADN'T BEEN an easy day.

Sophia closed the drawer of the filing cabinet and stretched her arms up, rolling her head to release the tension in her neck. Apart from a visit to the vault first thing in the morning, she'd spent the day at her desk, cataloguing and describing each photograph she'd uploaded to her computer.

She could barely remember what she'd had for lunch but the crumbs on the plate confirmed she'd eaten the sandwich Anna had brought her. She swallowed the dregs of cold coffee left in the mug and grimaced.

What she could remember, in sharp detail, was the way Loukas's arms had felt, steadying her last night. And that jolt of awareness that had electrified her when her eyes had met his and she'd realised he'd felt it as strongly as she had.

It hadn't been an easy night, either.

The hot shower had stopped her shivering but it hadn't done anything towards calming the shakiness she'd felt inside. She'd lain in bed, unable to sleep, while her mind replayed their encounter, over and over again.

What if…?

There was no point in wondering what would have happened if he'd kissed her. Or, more shockingly, if she'd initiated a kiss herself.

She wouldn't have let it go any further, she told herself. She'd have stopped it right there. Before he'd tried to remove the towel. Before he could see the scar.

But she hadn't been able to convince herself. The reaction between them had been so sudden and so visceral, and she had no other experience to compare it with. She'd never felt anything like it before.

The bright glare beyond the window had softened and she shut down her computer, locked the doors and headed out.

She needed fresh air, natural light and distance between her and this villa, with its extraordinarily rare contents and its enigmatic owner.

Loukas.

She wanted to know everything about him, but she felt that the less she knew about him, the safer she would be.

He was rich, beyond her sphere of imagination. He had the looks of an avenging angel. He was complicated and damaged. And he was her *client*.

He was not, *definitely* not, for her.

She left by the heavy oak door, running her

fingers over the smooth brass of the lion's head, as she closed it behind her.

The rocky track that led from the harbour to the front door continued, as a path, up the hillside behind the house. Sophia shaded her eyes with a hand and could see that it led to what seemed to be the highest point on the island.

She began to climb, pacing herself and stopping after five minutes to rest. She turned to admire the view that stretched out over the sea below. An afternoon breeze ruffled the surface of the water, whipping up choppy little waves with white caps.

In the distance, a sailing boat heeled, hauled close to the wind.

Stephanos was a tiny figure working on the deck of the *Athena*, where she lay at the quayside.

Sophia climbed a little further, relishing the silence. Bushes of oregano and thyme almost smothered the path in places, releasing their pungent scents into the warm air as her legs brushed against them. She picked a sprig and rubbed the leaves between her fingers.

Finally she reached a group of boulders on the summit of the hill.

She clambered up onto the biggest one she could manage and stood, taking in the views in every direction. Then she sat down and stretched out her legs on the sun-warmed rock. The muscles of her right thigh ached a little and she massaged them, pressing her thumb along the scar.

She saw him leave the house and begin to climb towards her. She'd told herself she didn't need to see him, it would be easier not to, after what had happened last night. But watching him approach gave her time to prepare what she might say to him. And time to tame the betraying flutter of excitement low down in her stomach.

You're here to do a job. The only acceptable attitude is a professional one.

'Sophia.'

He'd stopped a distance away, not yet at the top of the slope, fists resting on his hips.

She leaned back on her hands and waited.

'May I join you?'

Sophia nodded. 'I think this boulder is big enough for both of us.' She turned her head slightly away from him as he climbed easily up next to her. She could avoid looking at him, but she couldn't avoid his scent: a subtle blend of lemon and pine, and a hint of sweat. She shifted her position, adjusting her opinion of the size of the rock. Suddenly, it felt too small.

She dropped her eyes and crossed her right ankle over her left. Glancing up through her lashes, she saw the breeze lifting his black hair off his forehead, blowing it back, revealing a thread of silver running through the ebony. He sat with his legs bent, resting his arms on his knees, looking out at the horizon.

The hand nearest her rested, bronzed and long-fingered, against the denim of his jeans.

She swallowed and looked away. 'Were you watching me?'

'I saw you leave the house and take this path.' He nodded. 'From the study window.'

'If you'd wanted to talk to me, you could have come to find me in the office, with my head in the catalogue.'

'I was concerned about where you were going. I wanted to make sure you were safe.'

'Do you mean you wanted to make sure I wasn't going swimming in the sea on my own?' The breeze blew a lock of her hair across her face and she lifted a hand to tuck it behind her ear. 'Because you don't have to worry about that. I listened to what you said. And I know you're right.'

She thought she sensed some of the tension he carried with him seep out of his muscles and he relaxed slightly.

'Good. Thank you. I did think you might be going swimming but then I saw you turn this way.'

'But there's no swimming up here. Why did you follow me?'

'The path is steep, and it can be dangerous if you're not familiar with the terrain. And your leg…'

Sophia glanced down at her legs and then back

at Loukas. 'My leg is fine, most of the time. Last night was—'

He interrupted her. 'About last night… I apologise. It was…not what I intended to happen. Not at all.'

'No. But thank you for preventing my fall. As you said, I could have hurt myself.'

'You were already hurting.'

The breeze caught the edge of her gingham skirt. She lifted a hand and smoothed it down, trapping it under her palm.

'Not as much as it would have hurt if I'd cracked my head on the marble tiles in the pool. It's an ache rather than proper pain, and I'm used to it. It doesn't often let me down like that. Not any more.'

'What happened?'

'I was still a little tired from the journey. I'd been sitting all day. Then I possibly over-exercised it and got a little cold…'

'No. I mean, what *happened*? To your leg.'

It wasn't something she talked about. She'd dealt with it. It had taken a lot of time and a huge amount of determined self-belief and rehabilitation, but she'd reached a place of acceptance. And then she'd put it in a box in her mind and turned the key. Along with never knowing either of her parents and wishing she'd had a normal childhood, it was something she'd had to come to terms with. The alternative would have been self-pity and bitterness, and for Sophia that wasn't an option.

So faced with Loukas's question, she could either tell him it was something she only discussed with her physiotherapist, or she could offer him the quick, sanitised version of the accident. Last evening she'd experienced his questioning and, somehow, she felt he wouldn't be satisfied with the first option so she decided on the second.

She drew in a lungful of the salt- and herb-laden air. 'It was an accident. I collided with a London bus, at a junction.' It was a flippant way of describing the trauma of the catastrophic accident. It had been a wet day, a slippery road, blinding spray. The police report had concluded that neither she nor the bus driver were to blame.

'You were a pedestrian?'

From the corner of her eye she saw him turn to look at her.

'No.' She shook her head. 'I was riding my bike, to a rehearsal. My helmet protected my head. My thigh was not so lucky.'

She risked a glance at his face. He looked appalled. He shifted a little on the rock and glanced down at her crossed legs, hidden by the folds of her skirt.

'I'm so sorry, Sophia. How is it?'

'Oh...' she shrugged '...it's fine...it was a while ago, now. About five years...' She stopped, because she knew she wasn't being truthful.

She'd learned to be flippant and to brush questions aside.

'And how are *you*?'

Suddenly it felt important to be honest with Loukas. He was properly concerned about keeping her safe. And most people assumed she was okay since her limp was slight. They wanted to know the details of the accident and the injury, and whose fault it had been, not the state of her mind.

'Sophia?'

'I have a titanium plate in here.' She patted her thigh. 'It holds it all together. Now it's simply a part of me. If it hadn't happened, I wouldn't have my career at Marshalls. I wouldn't be here.' She made a wide, sweeping gesture with her arms. 'And it's so beautiful.'

'You're brave, Sophia, to have such a positive attitude.' He stretched out his legs next to hers and leaned back on his hands.

'I wasn't brave at the time. I was petrified. I thought I was going to die, right there, under the bus.'

'You were trapped under the bus?' His voice was quiet. 'For how long?'

She nodded. 'I don't know. They thought they'd have to perform surgery before they could get me out, but eventually they managed to extract me. Then they were convinced I'd lose the leg, but I had an amazing surgeon. He and his team did their best to save it, and their best was good enough.'

'It must have taken months…years…for you to get where you are now.'

She lifted her shoulders. 'It's ongoing. I have days when I feel the effort of having to do certain things. But then I also see improvements. I do my exercises and stay positive, as much as possible. I owe it to the doctors and nurses who cared for me to do the best I possibly can. And I was lucky.'

'Lucky?'

'I didn't die. They saved my leg. I can walk, run, climb, swim…'

His presence beside her heightened all her senses. His arm was close to hers, his long fingers almost touching her hand. She felt a sense of relief at having told him. She could swim in the pool or sunbathe on the beach now, without waiting for his shock at seeing her disfigurement. With luck, he wouldn't look away. And he hadn't picked up on the one slip she'd made.

'What was the rehearsal you were going to?'

The question hit her like a blow. She hadn't meant to say that, but she'd talked herself right into this.

She pulled up her legs and wrapped her arms around her knees, fixing her eyes on the horizon. The sailboat had hoisted a blue-and-red-striped spinnaker and was racing across the sea, running before the wind.

Sophia wished she could run from this conversation.

'Sophia?' The question was soft but probing.

'It was…*Swan Lake*. I was a ballet dancer. So, you see, I can do all those things, but the one thing I lived for, which was my passion, I can't do. Dancing gave me a sense of freedom and release when I was a child and adolescent. I'd joined the after-school ballet club in primary school and then I won a scholarship. In a ballet class I wasn't the girl with no parents. I was the same as everyone else. And I wasn't brave about losing that. When I knew I wouldn't dance again, I wanted to die.'

To her horror she felt her throat thicken with tears. Her eyes prickled. She never cried. Not any more. It was pointless and self-pitying. A waste of energy, when she had so much to be grateful for.

She raised the hand nearest to Loukas and wiped her index finger under her eyes, hoping he wouldn't notice the tears on her cheeks.

But those intense, dark eyes saw it all. She felt his hand touch her shoulder. The warmth of his compassion seeped through the cotton of her tee shirt and imprinted on her skin. She remembered how he'd held her steady the night before. How their eyes had sought each other out and the chemistry that had seemed to wrap around them, binding them together. How she'd felt as if she belonged, even though she'd never properly belonged anywhere.

His arm slid across her shoulders and pulled her against his side, holding her lightly, and she knew she could move away if she wanted to.

She didn't want to. She wanted to stay there, leaning into the powerful, solid shape of him. She swiped her hand across her eyes and shook her head. His hold slackened at once, but she pressed closer to him, dropping her cheek onto his shoulder.

'I…I'm sorry. I don't cry. Except…'

'Except sometimes?' He lifted her hair away from her face and tucked it behind her ear. 'I think it's okay to cry, sometimes, Sophia.'

She shook her head again. 'Except you've managed to get through my defences, somehow, and so I feel vulnerable.'

'Ah.'

'I never talk about it. Not ever. So I don't know how this happened. It's nothing to do with you and it doesn't affect how well I do my job.'

He circled her wrist with his free hand, then closed his fingers over hers and brought them to rest on his chest. She gulped, swallowing a sob, determined to subdue her emotions with the iron fist of control she normally used on them. It had always worked before.

'Why don't you talk about it?'

A tremor ran through her, and he pulled her closer.

'Because nobody wants to talk about things like that. It makes them uncomfortable. People didn't know how to deal with it. I think they were afraid I'd cry, and they wouldn't know what to say, so I was determined I never would. Not in front of anyone.'

'Surely the hospital offered some sort of counselling. Your grandparents...'

'They were both in a care home by then. I don't think they even noticed when I didn't visit for a while. And I refused to talk to a therapist. I just couldn't begin to share the turmoil that was going on in my head. Therapists can only help if you *want* help, and I didn't want it. Or pity. The nurses and doctors were sympathetic and very kind, but they're much too busy, anyway. I couldn't burden them with anything more.'

His fingers were making small circles on her shoulder, and she wanted him to go on doing that, for ever. It formed a connection between them, a gesture of comfort that was far greater than the slight movement should have been.

'You must have had friends in the ballet company. A...partner? Surely they visited you? Helped you?'

She nodded, her cheek rubbing against the soft cotton of his shirt.

'Yes. He...they did visit but I pushed them

away. They didn't have the words to deal with what had happened to me. It was a dancer's worst nightmare. I didn't belong with them any more. I'd never had a family, but I'd found one in the dance company. Then, within the space of a few seconds, I didn't belong to it any more. I was on the outside and I didn't want to be looking in.'

'And "he"?'

'He… Daniel…wanted to be supportive. He tried, but he…couldn't bear to look at my injured leg.' Her smile was tight. 'That's not a good basis for a relationship. I told him I was fine, but he didn't wait around to find out if that was true. He was a rising star. He didn't want to be held back by a disabled partner. I told him I'd come to terms with it, that I would make a new life. But inside, I was torn apart. I'd lost my career, my… partner, my family, and my future, all at once. A few of my friends tried to keep in touch but I shut them out. They live for dancing, as I had done, and I didn't want to be the one having to live without it.'

'Held back?' He hissed, *What a selfish…'*

Sophia shook her head. 'I couldn't blame him. Most people don't like seeing the scar.'

'How did you get from there to what you do now? It feels like a big leap.'

'Someone changed things for me.'

'You met someone else?'

'No. Not that sort of someone.' She shrugged

and thought she felt a little of his tension release. 'I don't think that's going to be easy, or even possible, for me. My grandfather had a friend who used to visit him. He was a historian whom he sometimes asked for advice. He had no children of his own but took an interest in me and used to include me in the conversations they had.'

She smiled. 'He said that I had "a good eye". He heard about the accident and came to see me. At first, he just sat by my bed and talked, although I wasn't very good company. He never once mentioned the fact that my dancing career was over. Then he began to bring in journals for me to read, art and antiques magazines, some auction catalogues. He'd page through them then ask my opinion on a picture or piece of porcelain. Over the weeks and months of recovery and rehab I began to look forward to his visits and I began to want to be able to give him opinions, answer questions.

'Of course, I know now that he knew all the answers already and had his own firm opinions, but he steered me in the direction of something else I could develop a passion for and which I grew to love. I try to see it as having changed the burden of my injury into the gift of my new career.'

'Do you still see him?'

Sophia nodded, again. 'I'm so grateful to him. He denies that he saved my life. He says the paramedics and the team at the hospital did that, but he saved me from becoming embittered, and I think that is almost as important. All the saving the medics did would have been for nothing if I'd chosen to waste my energy on self-pity and bitterness.'

She smiled against his shirt. 'I'm sorry I've offloaded my story onto you. I'm not a weak person, usually. You just caught me out.'

'I'm glad I did. I can tell you're not weak. You're amazingly strong.'

'Thank you. Now...' Sophia raised her head from his shoulder and straightened her back. Her eyes slammed into his and the emotion in them made her breath hitch. She pushed her hand into his chest, her fingers closing round the front of his shirt. 'Loukas...'

'Mmm,' he muttered. 'You're strong and a good example, and so beautiful.' He released her hand and her fingers tightened, winding themselves into the cotton and then, shockingly, feeling the skin of his chest beneath them, its smoothness slightly roughened by a dusting of hair.

Her hand stilled as twin flames of emotion lit his eyes.

'Loukas... I...'

'Yes,' he murmured as she lifted her face towards him.

Her lips were soft beneath his. He slid his fingers through her hair to cup the back of her head and hold her where he needed her, to give him maximum access to her yielding mouth. Her hair, he thought, was exactly as soft and silky as it looked. He circled his fingers, massaging the back of her head while his other hand stroked across the flushed skin of her cheek, and along the curve of her jaw, moving down to brush over her collarbone.

He could stay like this for hours. His mind slowed, his senses completely engaged by the feel of her lips, her light floral scent and the quick, erratic beat of the pulse under his fingers at the place where her shoulder curved into her neck.

She was delicate, damaged, yet so strong. His heart squeezed at the thought of the pain she'd suffered, the loneliness, and the seed of determination she'd cultivated to allow herself to survive and grow.

He'd wanted this. He'd wanted to feel her soft, full mouth beneath his, to taste the sweetness of her lips, but now he wanted more. A rush of desire threatened to sweep him away, beyond the reach of his self-control, but he didn't want to frighten her. He fought to keep the kiss gentle and restrained and, before he lost the battle, he lifted his lips from hers, steadying her head in his cupped hand.

But then she made a small sound in her throat. It was a sound of need and want and it wiped his mind. Her hand slid over his shoulder and up into his hair, gripping it between her fingers, pulling his head down to cover her mouth again.

He felt her tense under his hands, pushing towards him as if she never wanted him to let her go. Her mouth moved urgently, and he parted her lips with his, sliding the tip of his tongue into the sweet warmth.

The world receded, leaving nothing but acute sensation. The kiss became wilder, bolder as they explored each other. Loukas moved his hands over her lithe body, and gathered her against him, running his fingers down her spine and feeling her gasp under his mouth as he touched a sensitive spot, under her shoulder blades. He felt her hands slide under his shirt and his skin shivered as her fingers splayed across his shoulders and down to the small of his back.

With an effort that felt superhuman, he dragged his mouth from hers, ignoring her moan of protest. He pulled her head against his chest, trapping it there with one hand while the other stroked her back.

Her wide blue eyes were unfocussed and dreamy.

'Loukas,' she whispered.

'I need to stop,' he muttered. '*We* need to stop. Another minute and we…'

Her eyelids dropped and her breathing began to steady. He stroked a hand over her hip and smoothed her skirt over her thighs, feeling the ridge of the scar beneath his fingers.

Then he saw the moment when reality dawned. Her eyes fluttered open, and she sat upright abruptly, pushing his hand away, pushing herself away from him.

She pulled her legs up, hugging her knees.

'Don't,' she said. 'Don't touch my leg. I don't...'

'I'm sorry. I was covering your legs with your skirt, and yes, I felt the scar, but I didn't touch it. I wouldn't...'

'Nobody wants to touch it. I think it scares people.'

'It doesn't scare me.'

The look she threw him was sharp. 'Really? How did this happen?' She glanced around, as if realising where they were, processing what had happened.

He pressed a hand to his forehead. 'I...don't know. I wanted to kiss you, very much. I needed to, and then...you simply take my breath away.'

She shook her head, her hair flying around her face, confusion clouding her eyes. Then she slid off the smooth boulder, onto the rough ground, landing lightly on both feet. She looked back at him, shading her eyes against the low sun. 'Will you need to kiss me again? Because I don't think...' Her voice faltered.

He felt raw, as if she'd ripped a layer of protection from him and taken it with her. He wanted her back next to him. It had felt right, and he'd never expected anything to feel right on Alysos again. It calmed him, smoothed the jagged edges of memory. He suspected it could become addictive.

It seemed she was waiting for an answer, and he tried to drag his scorching thoughts away from the memory of her lips against his, and her body in his arms, to remember what the question had been.

Not need to kiss her again. The hell he could promise that.

'I'm not sure about that,' he said. 'I can't promise. Will you want to kiss me?'

'No. I don't know...'

She spun round and started down the path, her steps as light and sure as a dancer, even though she wasn't a dancer any more.

Then she spun to face him again, walking backwards.

'I've told you my story, Loukas,' she called. 'You'll have to tell me yours.'

'Sophia!'

He called after her, anxious that she might lose her footing and fall. The slope was steep and the path treacherous. If she fell... But if she stopped and came back he'd have to make up some question about dinner, or the catalogue.

She spun again and her pace didn't falter. She held up a hand, palm flat, to show she'd heard him, or it could just have been a 'stop' sign, but she kept going, surefooted, down the hillside.

Loukas watched her. She was brave, he thought, and determined.

The story of her life, up until now, was heart-breaking, but affirming at the same time.

The same could not be said of his.

CHAPTER SIX

SOPHIA DID NOT slow her pace until she reached the oak door of the villa. Twice she'd stumbled, thinking she would fall. Her heart raced and she'd begun to sweat, as she almost ran down the hillside, desperately needing privacy.

Loukas had called after her, but she'd pressed on, only acknowledging his voice with a raised hand.

She'd said far too much, and the situation had almost slipped from her control. She'd tried to snatch it back, flinging a light-hearted remark at Loukas as she'd left him.

She hadn't felt light-hearted, at all.

Her behaviour shocked and horrified her.

Nobody needed to know the sorry details of her life. Oversharing was self-indulgent, in her opinion, and she had never engaged in it, until today. And as if spilling her heart out to Loukas weren't bad enough, she'd *cried*? Could she have done a better job of humiliating herself? She didn't think so.

Her rating must have hit rock-bottom with him. She wondered if he'd want her to be replaced by another employee from London. Someone with more distance and less emotion.

And then there was that kiss.

Embarrassment made her cheeks flame, but her bold fingers, not embarrassed at all, strayed to her lips as she remembered.

It had grown wild, quite quickly, but that wasn't the problem. It had been intense, erotic and…she'd wanted it to go on for ever. Her shame came from the way she'd pulled his mouth down to hers, when he'd tried to stop. And from the re-alisation that *he'd* had the self-control to finish it.

Because she hadn't.

She'd been jolted back to reality when she'd felt his fingers smooth over her thigh. That was always going to bring her crashing back to earth.

It had taken her years to begin to be comfort-able with the livid stripe. She didn't know if she'd ever be ready for someone else's touch on the damaged skin, after witnessing Daniel's appalled recoil, and Loukas had come just too close, even if it had been unintentional.

She walked through the cool villa, across the drawing room, where the closed shutters shielded the room from the afternoon sun, and out onto the terrace. The sparkling water of the pool looked inviting, but she skirted it and reached her suite.

Relief wrapped around her as she closed the door behind her, shutting herself in.

The next time she saw Loukas, she'd suggest that she was fine working on the catalogue on her own. Anna and Stephanos could take care of her, while he could return to Athens, where he preferred to be, and their paths need not cross again. Fending off the emotions his presence stirred up was too difficult.

She was sure he'd agree that returning to Athens was the best thing to do. He was probably trying to work out how not to see her again, at this very moment.

How to get out of telling her about his childhood. He'd already insisted that he never spoke of it. What had possessed her to fling down that gauntlet? She hoped he'd accept it was not meant to be serious.

She felt fragile as blown glass, and emotionally drained. She didn't know how she could face him again. His compassion and gentle touch had stripped her of the defences she'd wrapped round herself for years.

But then there'd been nothing in her head except the need to surrender to the feel of his mouth on hers and of hard male muscle and wide shoulders under her hands. Desire, which she'd denied herself for so long, had ambushed her and it had been as unstoppable as an avalanche, until he had wrenched his mouth from hers.

Another hot rush of humiliation flashed through her. She was the cool expert, sent from London to undertake the most important job Marshalls had ever had, and she'd been willing to blow it out of the water.

Because if Loukas hadn't stopped that kiss…

Sophia limped to the bathroom, her damaged thigh protesting at the headlong way she'd descended the hill. The mirror showed cheeks flushed with hectic colour, and wide eyes. She splashed cold water over her face and counted through several deep, controlled breaths to try to steady her heartbeat. This sense of disarray was simply the result of her uncontrolled dash down the hill, she tried to tell herself.

She needed the distraction of work.

She pulled a towel off the rack and dried her face, and remembered she'd left her laptop in her office. Earlier, she'd been in such a hurry to leave the confines of the villa, she hadn't thought of returning it to her room. How ironic, she thought, that it had been the persistent memory of being in his arms last night that had driven her out, and straight back to him.

Was it worth retrieving her laptop and taking the risk of running into Loukas? Right now, the thought of seeing him again, so soon, filled her with confusion. She needed time to process her thoughts and to calm her body's responses, which seemed determined to dance beyond her control.

She glanced in the mirror again. Her slightly swollen, sensitised lips could not be blamed on anything other than the ravages of Loukas's mouth, and her desperate response to it. She patted on some lip balm, reliving that kiss, again.

This wasn't helping. She seriously needed her computer, to bury herself in the complications of the catalogue and the wording of a description of a particular painting that she'd been trying to get right. That was the only way she'd be able to push the thoughts of what had happened between her and Loukas into the background. She didn't bother pretending she'd ever banish them completely.

She slipped out of her door and kept to the shadow of the wall that separated the terrace from the small grove of ancient olives beyond it. Stephanos was walking between the trees, and he raised a hand in greeting when he saw her. She acknowledged him and then entered the villa through a side door, which she knew would bring her into the passage leading to her office.

It meant she'd have to pass Loukas's study, but that felt less exposed than walking the length of the drawing room, along the passage and past the main front door.

Her laptop was on the desk where she'd left it and it took only a moment to pick it up, gather up her notebooks, and leave again.

With her arms full, she tried to open the door

from the passage, but the pile of notebooks slithered from her grasp and cascaded onto the tiled floor in an untidy heap. She knelt down to gather them up and heard Loukas's study door open.

She saw his scuffed leather boat shoes first. Her gaze travelled over his ankles, up the long length of his legs, encased in the faded denims he'd worn all day.

Her eyes stopped at the open neck of his shirt. One button was missing, and the fine cotton was creased where her fist had clung onto it. She swallowed. Her mouth was dry.

'I heard you come in.' He glanced along the passage.

'Yes. I need my computer and I didn't want to disturb—'

'Sophia.'

She stood up, clutching the books in an untidy bundle. 'I need to work…'

'It's okay. Please don't hide away.'

'I'm not hiding. I'm going to work in my suite. I'm sorry. About this afternoon.' *Liar.* She'd do it again, which was why she had to keep away from him and keep her sanity intact. 'I…know how important privacy is to you. I've invaded your personal space. You won't like that.'

'That's for me to decide, don't you think? Let me help you with those.' He reached for the notebooks.

'Thank you.' His fingers brushed against hers and she let go of the books.

'I'll carry them to your suite and then leave you to work.'

At her door he handed them over.

'Thank you.'

'Dinner is at eight.'

Sophia backed into her suite, balancing the notebooks on top of the laptop.

'Oh, thank you, but wouldn't you prefer to dine alone?' She stopped, took a breath, and continued more slowly. 'Actually, I was going to say that you could easily return to Athens now. I'll be fine with Anna and Stephanos and I know you prefer to be there.'

His eyes were on hers, steady and intense.

'I feel I understand you a little, now. And I enjoy your company.'

'You don't need to understand me. You just need to be happy with the work I'm doing.'

He backed away, shoving his hands into the pockets of his jeans. 'On the terrace at eight. I'll see you there.'

'I don't think—'

'And right now,' he said as he turned, 'the idea of returning to Athens doesn't appeal to me. At all.'

CHAPTER SEVEN

THE IDEA OF returning to his study didn't appeal to him, either. It was a dim, sombre room, filled with memories that would intrude on his thoughts. And he needed to think. So he lifted the latch to the wooden gate in the rough white wall and left the wide, marble terrace and pool behind him.

He hadn't ventured into the olive grove since his return. As a boy, he'd loved the days when Christos had suggested to his tutor that they take their books outside, to sit amongst the old trees. Out here, his tutor would teach him about the shrubs and grasses that grew on Alysos, identify wildflowers and link them all to the ancient Greek myths, which he loved to read.

He sat on the scrubby grass in the shade of the trees. They'd been here for hundreds of years and would grow for many hundreds more, if properly cared for. The gnarled wood of their trunks and branches invited stroking, the dusty green leaves created sparse shade, but it was the fact of their age that he loved. Their steadfastness had always given him a sense of security and now he searched for that, again.

It was a long time since he'd felt truly comfortable anywhere but in his penthouse in Athens. Twenty-four hours ago, he'd been desperate to escape Alysos and return to his private space, overlooking the Acropolis, but now he wasn't so sure. Sophia's presence had dispelled some of the malevolent memories he'd expected to plague him here, stripped others of their potency.

But not all of them.

At first, she had reminded him too sharply of that other woman who'd captured all of Christos's attention. But that had dimmed as they'd talked. And since this afternoon he felt as if his brain had been wiped of all memory except that of the minutes they'd spent in each other's arms on a sun-warmed rock on the top of the island.

Her mouth under his, soft and yielding but becoming urgent with desire, the dart of her tongue, which sent arrows of sensation singing through him, her pulse picking up a hectic beat beneath his fingers and her lids dropping as her blue eyes lost focus and she gave herself over to the moment, then the little sounds she made in her throat. She had driven him to the very edge of his control.

It made him deeply uneasy. His scope of experience did not encompass dealing with these complicated emotions. He'd never had to address them before. He wasn't sure he even recognised them.

He realised he was gazing at the sea, without the usual creep of sickening fear, because his mind was occupied with thoughts of Sophia.

She'd shared her innermost private feelings with him. She'd bared her soul. He didn't feel worthy of the trust she'd placed in him.

After she'd run, he'd remained on the rock, wishing her back, wanting to kiss her again. He'd wondered if talking to him, even though she hadn't meant to, had enabled her to shed some sort of burden. He thought she'd shocked herself, but he hoped she wasn't regretting it.

He wanted to ask her. He needed to know it had helped.

She had turned and flung that challenge at him. He didn't want to shrug it off. Sophia was strong and brave and what she'd done had taken courage.

He felt the need to reciprocate. He wanted to share his past with her. It was something he'd never been able to do, with anyone. Christos had coaxed him to talk. He'd managed to help him to address his fears, but he hadn't been old enough to articulate his innermost feelings. And when Christos had died, he'd screwed down the lid on those feelings as tightly as his eight-year-old self had allowed.

Listening to Sophia, he'd felt something shift. His attention, always tightly focussed on the task of suppressing his emotions, had moved to her, and suddenly it felt as if those emotions were ready to be revealed, if he could find the courage to do it.

He felt the strength and bravery in the things she'd said. When he'd remarked that she was a good example, he'd meant it. She was a good example for him, and he was going to do his best to follow it.

He lay back on the spiky grass and folded his arms behind his head, content, for the first time in years, to lose himself in thought, rather than in spasms of guilt and bitter regret.

When a waft of cool air disturbed him, blowing over his skin, he opened his eyes to a darkened sky. Clouds, which had hovered on the horizon all day, had boiled up and obscured the sun. Despite the telltale, unsettled breeze, the air felt sultry.

In the distance, a squall raced over the inky sea, ruffling the sullen, glassy surface in its wake.

Loukas got to his feet and stretched, pushing a hand through his hair. A storm was brewing in the unsettled air. The familiar cold finger of dread traced the line of his spine. His palms felt clammy. He tried to blot out the image of the angry sea, boiling beneath the thunder and lightning, the lashing rain and huge swells that storms brought.

It was all in his imagination, he told himself. It was just a storm. It didn't mean anything.

* * *

The storm broke as night fell. A stark flash of lightning stabbed the dark sea, illuminating the white crests dancing on the wave tops.

Seconds later, the first crash of thunder ripped through the charged air.

Anna had taken the decision to move dinner off the terrace. She slid the doors closed against the weather and set up a table near the floor-to-ceiling windows.

Loukas stood in the drawing room, his body braced, as nature unleashed her fury all around him, firing off her first salvo in the battle between summer and autumn. As eight o'clock approached he focussed his attention on the corner of the terrace where Sophia would appear.

If she came.

As the first fat, shiny drops of rain splashed onto the marble and into the pool, he pulled back a section of the sliding doors and stepped outside. Each fork of lightning was more intense and each clap of thunder more deafening than the last as the storm raced across the sea towards Alysos.

Gritting his teeth, he ducked his head, sprinted around the pool and along the side of the terrace and banged on Sophia's door.

It opened almost immediately, and Sophia stood behind it, wide-eyed.

'What's wrong? Has something happened?'

'No. Nothing's wrong…' He was glad he'd

swapped his faded denims and the creased shirt, which was now missing a button, for black jeans and a fine-knit black sweater because Sophia had changed, too.

He stepped inside, out of the rain, which was rapidly becoming a downpour, and she closed the door against the storm.

He took a moment to absorb how stunning she looked.

Black leggings showed off her shapely legs and the colour of her thigh-length silk kaftan matched the colour of her eyes exactly, only he couldn't decide which was the more intense shade of blue. Her shiny blonde bob brushed her shoulders, and a simple silver chain gleamed around her neck.

If he could get enough oxygen into his constricted lungs he'd have a chance of getting his brain to function.

'You look beautiful.' She did. She looked breathtaking, but immediately he wished he could take the impulsive words back. He might scare her. What if she changed her mind and refused to have dinner with him?

But she simply dipped her head, avoiding his gaze. 'Thank you. Why are you here? Has dinner been cancelled?'

Was that a note of hopefulness he detected in her voice? She probably really did not want to see him but felt it would be unprofessional to refuse the invitation of a client, even if that client had held her so tightly and kissed her so hard, a matter of hours ago.

'Dinner on the terrace has been cancelled, but Anna has moved it inside. The terrace will be awash by now.' He gestured to the French doors, beyond which the rain now fell in sheets. 'I came to get you.' He shook his hair out of his eyes, sending a shower of drops flying. 'In case the rain put you off.'

For a split second the room was lit by a blinding white light and then the accompanying thunder cracked over their heads. Loukas flinched.

'I love storms, but I wouldn't want to be out in this one, especially amongst the rocks…'

Heat swept through him at the thought of the rock they'd been on that afternoon, and he saw, from her look of confusion, that her mind had leapt to the same place.

'If we run,' he said quickly, 'we'll get wet, but we'll soon dry out in the house.' He looked at her feet and saw she was wearing a pair of sparkly ballet pumps. The sight of them tugged at his heart. There'd been a time when shoes like those had been an essential part of her daily life. 'But we don't have to run, if it will be difficult for you…'

'I can run, Loukas.' She opened the door as the thunder crashed again. 'Let's go.'

It took less than a minute, but when they reached the sliding doors he found he was holding onto her hand. He pulled her inside and she turned to look at him, laughing, her eyes shining. Raindrops clung like diamonds to her hair and eyelashes.

'Are you all right? Not too wet?'

She slipped off her shoes. 'Only my shoes. They're soaked.'

He didn't want to let go of her hand, so he led her across the room to the table. Anna had lit candles and placed a posy of flowers in a silver vase in the middle. He pulled out a chair for Sophia.

'Anna will bring our meal in a few minutes. Drink?'

'This is so pretty, and so kind of Anna.' She settled into her chair, facing the window and the storm. 'Yes, please. We should drink a toast to Zeus. He's treating us to a display of his most impressive thunderbolts.'

By the time they'd finished their meal, the storm had moved on. An occasional flash of lightning lit the sky as the thunder grumbled in the distance.

Sophia raised her glass to swallow the last of her wine. 'The storm has almost run out of energy.'

Loukas had been distracted by her stream of conversation about the artworks she was finding in the vaults and the reaction she was receiving to the emails she was sending to London. He wondered if she'd been employing a delaying tactic, leaving him little time for what he wanted to say.

He had all night, and he wasn't going to be rushed. He could happily sit here for as long as necessary and watch her. The tilt of her head, the sometimes tiny, sometimes more extravagant movements of her hands, her occasional smile, were all mesmerising to him. He supposed her poise and expressiveness came from her ballet training, and it fascinated him.

He'd spent most of his life on the margins of socialising, observing rather than participating, and he was content to absorb her subtle sparkle and moments of seriousness. He was reluctant to bring it to an end but then he realised he did not know how to begin. It was he who was delaying.

How did you tell an almost-stranger something so personal? He thought back to the afternoon and Sophia's bravery and candour, and knew he had to try.

What if she suddenly wanted to leave? It was late and she must be tired. She might suggest postponing their discussion until the following day. She'd apologised for her outpouring of emotion. He wanted to try to balance it for her.

By tomorrow his courage might have deserted him.

Then suddenly she made it easy.

'Were you afraid of the storm, Loukas?' She put her glass down and clasped her hands together on the table. 'You were tense, but now that it's passed, you're more relaxed.'

He felt anything but relaxed. 'I don't enjoy storms. I can't relish them like you.'

Until this evening he would have considered that an understatement. He hadn't enjoyed the storm, but it hadn't held that intense power to terrify him, to torture him with flashbacks, to fill him with a sense of loss so profound it felt fathomless.

'Is there a logical reason for that?' The tilt of her head was slight. 'Is that part of your story?'

'You're very perceptive.'

She lifted her shoulders slightly. 'I spent most of my childhood observing. I haven't lost the habit.'

Loukas lifted the bottle of wine from the bucket at the side of the table, but she put her fingers over her glass.

'No, thank you.' The curve of her hair caught the glow of the candlelight as she shook her head. 'You're procrastinating.'

Her slight smile softened the admonishment, but he knew she was right. He needed to stop putting it off.

'It's difficult to talk about something I've never been able to discuss with anybody, but you showed me this afternoon that it can be done. All it takes is determination and courage.'

'I had neither of those qualities this afternoon. My determination to keep my story to myself and my courage both failed me. I talked, and I cried.'

'When I was four years old,' he said evenly,

'my parents both drowned in a storm.' He twisted in his chair and looked through the expanse of glass to the blackness beyond. 'Out there. Their boat capsized and they were trapped beneath it.' He turned back to face her. 'I've been afraid of storms ever since. And of water.'

He watched the colour leach from Sophia's face, leaving her deathly white. Her wide eyes shimmering with distress. She unclasped her hands and pressed them over her mouth, shaking her head.

Then she reached across the table and took one of his hands, folding her fingers around it.

'Loukas… I'm so, so sorry. And you were probably too young to have proper memories of them.'

He thought he should pull his hand away from hers, but the connection was powerful and he didn't want to break it.

'I…remember the day quite well. I wish I didn't.'

'You were *here*? Did you *see* what happened?'

'No. I wasn't here. I was *there*, on the boat with them.'

The grip of her fingers tightened.

'You don't have to tell me this, Loukas. It must be too painful for you.'

'Would you prefer me not to? It's distressing for you, too.'

'No. Not if it helps you to talk. But if it doesn't…'

Now that he'd started, he really wanted to get

this done. He hadn't expected it to be easy, but he'd thought he'd be able to do it. He recognised the first frightening signs of a panic attack.

He'd managed to control them for years, but something was slipping, and he was losing his grip on his emotions. His heartbeat felt loud and intrusive, and it kept getting quicker. The weight on his chest threatened to stop him from breathing, unless he concentrated on every inhalation and exhalation. Sweat pricked on his scalp.

Sophia's voice was low and steady when she spoke. 'Breathe, Loukas. You'll be okay. Breathe, and look at me.'

He found her blue eyes and stared into them. Her hand smoothed over his in rhythmic strokes and the world shrank to just the two of them, at this table. Perhaps, he thought, that was all he needed, but it wouldn't be what she needed.

With her free hand she picked up his glass of water and offered it to him. He took it and swallowed a mouthful, relieved when it didn't choke him. The glass rattled against the tabletop as he put it down.

'Thank you. I...' The symptoms began to recede. 'This hasn't happened for a while. I'm sorry.'

'Don't talk any more, if you don't want to.'

'I do want to. I need to. If you want to hear.'

She nodded. 'Okay. You were on the boat. What happened?'

'The storm blew up with little warning. We

were visiting Christos and he suggested we went for an afternoon sail. It was a breezy day and afterwards Christos blamed himself. He should have seen the storm coming. I couldn't swim so I was wearing a life jacket. That is why I survived.' He pulled a hand over his face. 'My father changed course, to get into the lee of another island, but the wind was too strong. The waves... I can remember the waves...were mounting. They clipped me to a safety harness while they went below to get life jackets for themselves, but it was too late. The wave that capsized the boat also swept me into the sea.' He took a deep breath, but his impeded lungs struggled to find enough oxygen. 'They were trapped, and the boat sank very quickly. The weight of water...do you know how heavy it is? I have nightmares about it, still.'

Sophia had gone very still, and he thought again how beautiful she looked, with her blue eyes and golden hair, in the candlelight. Goosebumps roughened her forearms and she shivered. He shouldn't be burdening her with this story. She'd had enough tragedy in her life already.

'And you?' she whispered. 'How long was it before you were found?'

'I remember the storm and my father clipping on the harness. He shouted something but I've never been able to recall the words. The power of the wave that washed me off the deck is what has stayed with me, but I have no memory of what happened next.

'I was rescued quite quickly. Christos had seen the boat capsize and had already called for help before it sank. The force of the wave had ripped the harness from the rail. Otherwise, I would have been pulled under, too.'

He watched Sophia's teeth close over her bottom lip. Her eyes sparkled with tears.

'I've always longed for a memory of my parents. Even just a fleeting one. But to live with the memories you have must be almost intolerable. To have lost them so suddenly and in such a brutal way...' She shook her head. 'What became of you?'

'Christos and my father had been close friends since childhood. He was my godfather, and he knew I had no other close family.' He glanced down to where their hands were linked across the table. 'He was kind and gentle. He did his best to replace my terrifying memories by telling me happy stories about my parents, while he himself must have been torn apart by grief at their loss and tortured by self-recrimination. I was the sole heir to my father's company.' He shrugged. 'I was a billionaire orphan at the age of four.' He shook his head. 'I was a liability, a kidnap target. But Christos never, ever made me feel like a burden.'

'But then he died,' she murmured.

Loukas swallowed and looked away, over Sophia's shoulder towards Christos's portrait where it hung, illuminated, on the wall alongside those of his ancestors.

'I remember that last summer quite well. I was eight. Christos had finally helped me to overcome my terror of water. He'd even managed to teach me to swim. I'd begun to think I'd be able to swim in the sea, one day.'

'That's why you don't swim.'

He nodded.

'Afterwards, I was sent to live with my tutor, at his sister's home in Athens. I was schooled at home, guarded by minders, but when I became a rebellious teenager I was sent away to a school in Switzerland where they were used to dealing with mega-rich, messed-up kids like me. Christos's lawyer told me he'd made me his heir when my parents died. I think it was another way of trying to compensate for what I'd lost. If he'd married and had his own family, I'm sure he would have changed his will.'

'Loukas, what happened to Christos?'

His head snapped up and he blinked, shocked by her sudden question. He tugged at his hand but she tightened her hold on his fingers.

'I will never,' he said, his voice harsh, 'talk about that.'

Her look was steady, her face still. 'Okay. But if you ever need to…'

'I won't.' He shook his head. 'I took a finance

degree in England and became qualified to run my father's business. I worked my way up, in other companies, and in other countries, but eventually I came back to join the company in Athens.' He shifted in his chair. 'These days, I could do a lot from home, but I prefer to travel.'

She still held his hand, and he knew he should break the contact now. He ran his thumb across her knuckles, stroking the soft skin. Her eyelids dropped, lashes sweeping down onto her cheeks.

'Is that because if you keep moving you never have to confront your feelings?'

'I confront them every day. They never leave me, wherever I am in the world.' He pinched the bridge of his nose between his fingers.

'It's easier to keep running.' Her voice was so soft he could barely hear her. He pushed an agitated hand through his hair.

'I'm not running away from anything. I'm doing a job. I like to stay in touch with the offices, all over the world. It's important to see people, face to face.'

'That sort of life may be good for business, but it leaves no opportunity to form a long-term relationship.' She raised her eyes again. 'I know you're a private man, but surely it's a lonely existence.'

'Relationship?' He said the word as if it were unfamiliar, or in a foreign language. 'I have no time or need for one.'

'You'll be glad to get back to Athens, then, to carry on with your life.'

He bit his lip, studying her. She seemed to be able to see into his soul and read the words written there. In reality, he could live his life any way he chose because an excellent team ran the business, worldwide, and he could keep in touch with his directors from anywhere. The idea of a relationship filled him with anxiety. He'd seen how fate could twist, in a split second, upending everything you loved and thought would last for ever and leaving you confused and lost, at the mercy of what other people decided was the right thing for you.

He pulled his hand from beneath hers and crossed his arms over his chest. 'Perhaps I will,' he said, 'if you think you'll be all right here, with Anna and Stephanos.' Returning to Athens felt impossible, but staying in Sophia's entrancing orbit would be dangerously beguiling and it would lead nowhere good. A fling that could last for a few days at the most would never satisfy a woman like her. She'd want it all—everything he could never give. She deserved so much more than a man like him.

'I'll be fine.' She dipped her head so that her hair slid in a curtain across her face, hiding her expression. 'I think I'll finish it more quickly than I first thought.'

'Good,' he said, even though disappointment

lodged, heavy, in his chest. 'Since I became old enough to understand it, the art collection has only ever felt like a burden.' He pushed his chair back and stood up. 'Once it's gone, I can leave the island in the care of Stephanos and Anna and when they wish to retire, I'll sell it.'

'Disposing of the art will be easy. Collectors will be falling over themselves to get a piece of it. Shifting your memories will be more difficult. You can't sell those.' She glanced up at him. 'Do you think it will make you happier?'

'I don't think I'll ever be happy, in the conventional sense.'

'After the accident, I thought I'd lost all chance of happiness and I had to confront that. I took a conscious decision to make my life the best it could be. My expectations have changed, but I'm trying to live the life I've been given as well as I can.'

He watched Sophia rise from the table and stand looking out at the sea. It lay, coal-black and shiny, under the broken moonlight, with little trace left of the storm. The smooth swells were larger than usual, and the spray from an occasional wave crashing against the harbour wall rose higher, but the rain had moved on and the wind had stilled. The moon rode high in the sky, clouds scudding across her face.

As he bent to blow out the candle, she turned from the window. The flame dipped and died, leaving the table in darkness.

'Loukas…'

But he'd done with talking. What use had it been? He'd thought it might make him feel better—that it would be cathartic—but instead he felt raw and on the edge of losing control.

He needed to escape.

He looked towards her, and she raised her chin and tucked her hair behind her ears, her eyes colliding with his.

Even in the dim light the connection was mindblowing. The chemistry bouncing between them felt powerful enough to spontaneously combust. Who needed the candle, he thought, when we could generate enough power between us to light up the whole of the Aegean?

He tried to crush that thought. He couldn't deal with this. He needed his energy to keep himself together. Sophia had worked some sort of rough magic on him, weakening his tough exterior, threatening to open him up to vulnerability.

He should have ignored her challenge to tell his story. His memories of the day his parents died were sketchy, but his imagination had filled in the gaps. Talking about it, putting the event into words, was the last thing he should have done, because it had brought the guilt, which he tried to keep buried, back to the surface to torment him.

He should never have survived that storm. The sea should have taken him, too.

CHAPTER EIGHT

Sophia had made two trips to the vaults to check. She'd searched every corner of the cavernous space. Until now she'd matched up every other artwork with its corresponding file in the catalogue. Whoever had organised it had been meticulous, which made this missing piece of sculpture perplexing. The file bulged with paperwork, but the object was nowhere to be found.

She hadn't seen Loukas since their dinner, three days ago. She assumed he'd returned to Athens.

The image of him leaning over the table to blow out the candle haunted her. The gleam of his ebony hair, the straight lines of his mouth and dark brows, the line of his jaw, were there, waiting for her, every time she allowed her mind to wander.

It wandered far too often. She wished she could see him again. For three days she'd expected to turn and find him observing her from the door or leaning on the balustrade of the terrace.

His revelations had shredded her emotions. She

longed to be able to help him, but he didn't want to be helped. He'd locked up his heart and thrown away the key.

She needed to find that key, or he'd spend the rest of his lonely life running from his traumatic memories.

And although she knew it was unethical and unprofessional, she longed, too, for that sense of belonging that being in his arms had brought her. Their kiss had set alight a part of her she hadn't known existed and, although she knew it was dangerous, her body ached for more.

To Loukas, it had been just another kiss, given because he thought it would make her feel better. And now he'd gone, retreated to Athens, to the remote man he'd been when she arrived. All she could do now was send him an email to see if he could shed any light on this missing piece of sculpture.

It was three hours before his reply dropped into her inbox, and when it did, she had to read it twice.

He was here, he said, and would have a look at the problem.

Sophia was still trying to process the fact that he was on the island when, five minutes later, he walked into the office.

She stood up, sending her chair spinning away from her, and stared at him.

'I…thought you'd gone back to Athens… Where have you been?'

The shadows under his eyes made him look as if sleep was a distant memory and his jaw was rough with stubble.

'You'd have heard the helicopter if I'd left. You know I avoid the sea. I've been…hibernating. I didn't feel like company.'

'I…I'm sorry I disturbed you. I can deal with this problem on my own. I'll email Sean. He's never short of ideas. There's probably a simple explanation.'

He held up a hand. 'Stop, Sophia. I don't feel like company, but I can try to help.'

She shook her head. 'No. Please don't stay. Really, I can manage it. You don't need…'

He ignored her and glanced at her desk.

'Show me.' He bent over the open file. 'Please.' It seemed like an afterthought.

Sophia's hands shook slightly as she pointed to the file. She pulled in a breath to steady them. The technique she'd learned to use, before going on stage, of focussing her attention on her breath still proved useful in stressful situations, and she used it now.

It didn't work while six feet three inches of the modern-day equivalent of Adonis leaned over her, his arm brushing her shoulder. A heavy lock of his hair fell over his forehead, and he frowned. A muscle in his jaw ticced.

He might not have shaved but he'd showered in something that smelled of pine and spice and

Sophia had to breathe again, and swallow, before she dared to speak.

When she explained the problem, her voice was husky.

Loukas straightened up and rocked back on his heels, pulling a hand over the back of his neck.

'I think I know where this is.'

Sophia retrieved her chair, eased herself down into it and spun round to face him.

'Really?' The end of the assignment was in sight. She thought she could finish in three more days, if no more problems like this one arose, and then she could leave.

She was an intrusion on Loukas's privacy. If he was avoiding her, he must want her gone.

The idea of leaving squeezed her heart.

'I'll show you.' He opened the door and held out his hand. 'Come with me.'

Sophia followed him along the wide passage, past the side door where, what felt like a lifetime ago, she'd tried to sneak in undetected to retrieve her laptop. His strides were long and quick, and she struggled to keep up with him. She saw tension stretched across his shoulders and in the way he moved. Whatever he'd been doing over the past three days, it hadn't involved relaxing.

The passage ended in a solid wooden door. A small brass plaque screwed to it read 'Private' in Greek and in English. Loukas removed a key card from the pocket of his jeans and slipped it into a slot in the door handle. He pushed the door open, and hesitated.

'This is my private apartment. It's where Christos and I lived. No visitors came through this door.'

Sophia stood back. 'If you'd rather I didn't come in...'

'It's the only way I can show you the sculpture. And since I'll be leaving the island in a few days, I don't see the problem.'

She followed him into a spacious hall and then through double doors into a large living room, furnished in a relaxed style of thirty years ago. Sofas that had been modern then but were probably described as mid-century now were arranged around a pale wood coffee table. Sliding glass doors in wooden frames opened onto a courtyard, wrapped by the building on all four sides.

Sophia walked to the open door and stepped outside.

Slender marble columns supported a wooden pergola on all four sides of the courtyard and the vine that climbed over it looked a century old. A few of its green, shade-giving leaves already showed a tint of autumnal orange. The deep veranda was dotted with comfortable chairs and a small table.

Geraniums in terracotta pots spilled pink blooms

onto marble tiles and several tall olive oil jars punctuated the space.

The musical sound of trickling water drew Sophia's attention to a smooth marble basin in the centre of the courtyard. Perfect pink waterlilies floated on its surface and on a plinth in the centre stood a marble statue of a Greek goddess.

Loukas paused. Sophia had her hands in the pockets of her cream linen crops and as he watched, she drew them out slowly. Her fingers were curled against the palms of her hands, and then she folded her arms. Her head tilted to one side as she took a few slow steps around the pool. He saw her narrow her eyes.

She continued her scrutiny, all around the statue, and stopped again in front of it. Head bent, she appeared to be studying her feet, but then she raised it again and glanced at him, over her shoulder.

He caught the blue of her eyes and the bright shimmer of her hair. It was almost midday and the shadows were stunted and dark.

He waited.

Her shoulders dropped as he heard her exhale, and she turned towards him.

'She's…exquisite.'

He stepped out of the shade of the colonnade, into the warm sunlight. The white walls dazzled, and he pulled a pair of sunglasses from his shirt pocket. He hadn't left the apartment for three days and his eyes were unaccustomed to the bright light.

'She is. Her perfect hands fascinate me. Look…' He extended an arm and ran a finger over the polished marble. 'They're like yours.'

'Are they?' Sophia held up her hands, smiling. 'I don't think I measure up to Aphrodite.'

'You think she's Aphrodite?'

'Yes. I think she's a Roman copy of the famous Greek original, sculpted by Praxiteles in the fourth century BC, the goddess of love and beauty.' Her hand hovered over the goddess' extended left arm. 'She's just reached out for her bath towel. She must have been bathing.' She pulled out her phone. 'May I?'

He nodded. 'Of course.'

Sophia circled the pool, photographing the sculpture from different angles and then sliding her phone back into her pocket. 'She was made to be viewed from all angles, so this is the perfect place for her.' She looked round, as if noticing the wider space for the first time. 'This is a beautiful courtyard. Thank you for allowing me to see it.'

He shrugged. 'No problem.' His gesture encompassed the space. 'That is the kitchen. I've been eating out here, when…when I've been on my own. And along those two sides are en suite bedrooms. All the rooms are only accessible through the courtyard. It's very secure.' He ushered Sophia back inside. 'Beyond the windows are sheer cliffs—you will have noticed from the top of the hill...' He hesitated, regretting bringing up the subject of their meeting on the hilltop. 'Perhaps you've noticed.'

Sophia nodded. 'And this part of the house was kept completely private?'

'Mmm. The rest of the house is big enough for entertaining. Christos threw epic parties, but no guests ever came through that door.' He glanced out into the courtyard. 'I'll have to consider how to remove Aphrodite from the pool and unite her with the rest of the collection.'

He had spent three days not seeing her. It had been hell.

Knowing she was there had tormented him. He'd wanted to find her and apologise for spoiling her evening with his selfish reminiscences, but he hadn't thought she'd want to see him.

And after apologising, the next thing he needed was to kiss her, again, like before, but for longer, and not on a rock at the top of a hill. A bed would do.

He couldn't think beyond that.

He'd told Anna and Stephanos not to disturb him and retreated behind the locked door to his private rooms, burying himself in work and pounding the treadmill in the small gym, sometimes in the dark hours of the night. When that hadn't helped, he'd lifted weights, punched his punchbag, but there was a limit to the number of cold showers he could tolerate. He'd reached that limit on day one, and since then his imagination had defeated all his efforts to suspend it.

He wasn't used to company, he told himself. She was a beautiful woman with a soft smile who seemed to be able to see into his damaged soul and unravel his secrets. What man would be able to resist her?

Her presence had altered the whole atmosphere of Alysos. It no longer felt like the desolate, lonely place it had become in his mind. Even from behind his locked door, he thought he could feel the change, but then he acknowledged that the change was in himself.

His avoidance tactics had been pointless. He'd forced himself to neither see her nor communicate with her, and almost believed he'd be able to fight his way through this. But from the second her email had pinged into his inbox he'd known he'd lost the battle. Refusing to acknowledge that his willpower had crumbled, he'd fought on for three more hours.

Then he'd uttered a string of Greek expletives, pleased that no one but himself could hear them, and cracked.

He ran a palm over his jaw, shocked at its harsh roughness. If he'd taken time to reason with himself, he would have acted no differently, but he might at least have shaved first.

Sophia was walking towards the door, and he

really, really didn't want her to leave. He'd only been with her for a few minutes, and he needed longer—much longer. He followed her, trying desperately to think of a way of stalling her departure.

'Is there anything you need?' he asked. He'd abandoned her for three days and she was probably just fine with that. If she needed anything she would have asked Anna, or Stephanos. She wouldn't need anything from him.

'I'm fine, thank you.' Her generous smile knocked the air from his lungs and coherent thought from his stressed brain. 'I'd like to deal with this—' she tapped her phone in her pocket '—and then I think I'll be able to finish up and get out of your way in a few more days. This whole assignment has gone much more smoothly than I'd anticipated.'

There were many words he could use to describe how the assignment was going, for him. Smooth was not one of them. The thought that he could try to derail it, make it last longer, occurred to him. He'd have to find a way.

'You're hardly in my way.' Her hand was on the door handle. 'I'm sorry I've been…unreachable… for the past few days. I was trying to resolve something. I…'

'No problem. I hope you've sorted out whatever it was.'

Not at all. And I don't know how I ever will.

She pulled on the door, and he held it open, resisting the crazy impulse to slam it shut, lock it and shred the key card. He at least had to make sure he saw her again, soon. Any remaining resolve to avoid her had dissolved in the warmth of her smile.

'Have you been swimming again?' An idea that would put him so far out of his comfort zone that he couldn't believe he'd even thought of it sprang into his head.

She looked startled. 'Yes, I have.' She held up her hand as he opened his mouth to speak. 'I took your advice and made sure that either Anna or Stephanos was nearby, as I promised.'

'That wasn't so much advice as a...*directive*.'

She raised her chin. 'Oh? Is that another way of saying it was an *order*? Because I don't—'

'But would you like to go to the beach?' he interrupted. The words were out there, before he had time to reconsider. The beach was his worst nightmare but now he thought the idea of not having a reason to see Sophia might take that top slot. He could avoid the beach, but once she was gone there'd be a gap in his life that would never be filled. 'I could come with you...'

Her eyes, blue as the summer sky, rested on him, questioning the question. She tilted her head. 'The *beach*? I'd love to go to the beach. It looks so beautiful, from up on the hillside.'

Suddenly the possibility of spending more time

with her felt like a gift. His tense shoulders relaxed, and he tried to breathe.

'What time will you be free, do you think?'

'I can stop work around five, but I'll have to check my emails later, to make sure I'm keeping up with the plans in London.'

'Sounds fine.' He tried to keep his reply neutral.

Sophia raised a hand in one of the expressive gestures that reminded him of a tiny bird taking flight, or of a butterfly, as she spun on her good leg and walked away, her golden hair swinging about her shoulders.

The door clicked shut and Loukas made his way back to the courtyard, feeling drained. He was right about her eyes. The sky above him was that exact same shade of blue. He dropped his gaze to the sculpture.

'Thank you, Aphrodite,' he murmured.

CHAPTER NINE

IT WAS AFTER five o'clock by the time Sophia sat back in her chair. She'd studied the detailed paperwork on the sculpture. She'd been right about it depicting Aphrodite, goddess of beauty and love. All that remained to look at was a sealed brown envelope, which had given the file its bulk. The word 'Personal' was scrawled in one corner. She'd decided not to open it.

Returning to her suite, she pulled on her bikini and a long shirt, slipped her feet into her sandals and draped a cotton wrap around her shoulders.

Loukas stood at the foot of the steps. She found it hard to believe he'd disappeared so completely for three days yet had been nearby all along. How hadn't she known? Or sensed his presence?

Obviously, he had wanted—needed—to avoid her. Did he regret kissing her or telling her about the death of his parents?

He raised a hand when he saw her, narrowing his eyes into the sun. His black hair was tousled, but he'd shaved since their meeting earlier.

The brisk breeze, which had cooled the island during the day, had dropped and the late afternoon was still. The harsh white light of midday had softened, taking the heat with it but leaving behind a mellow warmth. A gecko lay on a rock nearby, catching the last of the day's sunshine.

'Are you sure you want to go to the beach?' Loukas looked anxious and tense, as if he needed to get this over with.

He nodded. 'Let's go.'

He turned and strode off down the worn track. Tension radiated from his back and shoulders and in the way he ran a hand over the back of his neck. Sophia had an insane urge to call out to him, to tell him to stop, to stand and take a deep breath and admire the view, while she put her palms on his spine and massaged the knotted muscles until he relaxed.

'Loukas…'

He glanced over his left shoulder but kept walking, like a man on a mission.

Suddenly, Sophia thought she understood. He hated and feared the sea, and this would be an ordeal for him. He was determined to go through with it, but he had to keep the momentum going because, if he didn't, if he gave himself time to think, he might lose his nerve.

He wouldn't want to do that in front of anyone. Why he'd offered to bring her to the beach, when he didn't have to, was something she couldn't begin to understand.

They reached the quayside at the foot of the path and Loukas paused long enough for Sophia to draw level with him. She rubbed a hand over her thigh, massaging the tight muscles, and saw his frown of concern.

'I'm so sorry. I forgot that you... I was intent on getting here.'

'It's okay. I could tell you were in a hurry. It's good exercise for my leg.'

He shook his head. 'It was thoughtless of me. Would you like to rest for a minute?'

'No, let's keep going. Which way?'

He pointed to the left, where the path reappeared, climbing over the headland, which extended beyond the harbour.

Sophia stopped when she reached the ridge at the top.

'This is like everyone's imagined Greek island cove. Pristine sand, turquoise water and complete privacy. It's perfect.'

The sea hissed quietly as it washed over the white sand, curling around the boulders that dotted the beach. She could imagine that Zeus had gathered them all up in his giant fist, like marbles, and dropped them where they lay.

She jogged down the slope and slipped off her sandals, dumping them on the sand. Then she unbuttoned her shirt and let it slide off her shoulders, tying the wrap around her waist. She walked carefully down towards the water, making deliberate footprints in the crunchy sand. A ripple, warm and silky, washed over her feet.

Looking back up the beach, she saw that Loukas had stopped where she'd left her clothes. His eyes were fixed on her, and even from a distance she could see the tense alertness in his stance.

She wished she could help him. She'd love to dive into the crystalline water alongside him and swim out into the bay. His body...

She stopped that thought, trying to reimagine him dressed. All she was to him was an inconvenience. She turned and bit her lip, dropping the wrap on the sand and wading into the sea.

Tiny fish darted away, gleaming like quicksilver in the sunlight, as she dived into the water.

It was liberating. The gentle swells took her weight, supporting her, and she allowed the sea to rock her to its own timeless rhythm. High above her, in the azure sky, a bird wheeled and called as she drifted, thinking this was the nearest thing to flying she could imagine, and quite possibly the nearest place to paradise.

Loukas kept his eyes on Sophia. If he watched her, he'd know at once if she got into any difficulty. He didn't allow himself to wonder what he'd do about it if she did.

Anxiety made his throat close, and panic hovered on the edge of his awareness, threatening to take the first opportunity it could find to dig its claws into his mind and run away with it.

By the time he'd reached the edge of the sand she had already been at the water's edge. He'd seen her disappear beneath the surface as she'd dived in and he didn't breathe again until she surfaced, yards away from where he'd last seen her.

Would she hear him if he called? He didn't think she would.

He hated this. Hated that he couldn't control his response to the fear, or to Sophia, and hated that his behaviour was irrational.

He'd tried, so hard, to take himself back to the time when Christos had taught him to swim. He still remembered the kick of triumph he'd felt when he'd mastered it and swum the length of the pool, with Christos swimming backwards, just in front of him, ready to catch him if he foundered or panicked. He'd trusted Christos absolutely.

It was no use. When Christos had died, he'd felt as if he had been thrown into the deep sea and were sinking, no matter how hard he struggled to keep his head above the water.

Those feelings turned into nightmares, mixed up with his memory of his parents drowning. They still regularly disturbed his sleep.

He lost sight of Sophia as a swell rose between her and the beach. Then he breathed again when she reappeared. He wanted to call to her, to ask her to come out now. He didn't think he could do this for much longer.

What if her damaged leg grew tired? What if she suffered from cramp in her strong leg? What if…?

Then he saw her roll onto her stomach and begin to swim towards the shore, moving through the water with the smooth, long strokes he'd seen her use in the pool.

She walked up the beach towards him, limping slightly, her cotton wrap wound around her waist. Gathering up her hair in her hands, she squeezed the seawater out of it and then shook her head, releasing a spray of silver drops.

Her perfection was enough to bring him to his knees. The wet wrap clung to her and rivulets of water trickled down her legs. A faint breeze sifted across the beach and as she drew nearer, he saw goosebumps roughen her skin. She must be cold. His eyes moved over her, trying to imprint this image of her on his mind so that he could revisit it after she'd gone.

The cold had hardened her nipples beneath the fabric of her bikini top, and Loukas swallowed and dragged his eyes away from them, down over her flat stomach, to the curve of her hips and thighs. There was nothing about her he'd want to change.

'That was the best swim I've had in a long

time.' She laughed. 'In fact, the best swim, ever. I wish...'

He felt weak with relief that she was back with him, safe and unharmed.

'What do you wish, Sophia?'

'Oh.' Her face clouded, and her smile died. 'I wished you were swimming with me, but that was insensitive.'

She hitched the wrap up, tucking it under her arms, then sat down on the sand with her knees drawn up under the bright cotton and patted the place next to her.

'Sit down, Loukas. I want to spend a little time watching the sea change from its daytime to its evening colours.'

'I thought you needed to get back to check your emails.'

Loukas joined her on the sand, resting his forearms on his bent knees. He turned his head towards her. 'Is the paperwork in order?'

Sophia shrugged and the thin cotton slipped lower, revealing the swell of her breast. He found the tantalising glimpse more erotic than the sight of her in a wet bikini.

She wriggled her shoulders, hitching it back into place.

'Yes,' she said, slowly, 'but there's a sealed envelope in the file, marked "Personal". I didn't want to open it. I'll give it to you.'

Her nearness sent heat surging over his skin.

He wondered if she felt it, too. He glanced sideways at her, taking in her pure profile, the sensuous curve of her mouth, her hair tucked behind her ear.

He gripped his hands together, to keep them under control. She was more beautiful than Aphrodite, and she was warm and vivid, kind and compassionate. He wanted to tell her how he'd fought against the part of him that wanted to explore her mouth again, with his, and to feel her responsive body tighten under his hands. He wanted to hold her in his arms and share her warmth, feel her melt against him again.

Hell, he wanted all of her.

'You find this really difficult, don't you?' She turned her head and looked at his bloodless knuckles. 'You're completely stressed out.' She raised a hand and rested it over his.

He closed his eyes, briefly, unable to watch, but unable to remove his hand. Her touch was gentle but insistent, the pad of her thumb soft where it stroked the stretched skin.

'Sophia…'

'I'm sorry I let you bring me here. It was selfish of me. But try to relax. Everything's okay.'

He turned his hands and enclosed hers in their grip.

She raised her head. Her eyes darkened to a deeper blue, a spark of something that could have been apprehension firing briefly in their depths.

The chemistry between them, bottled up and denied for three days, simmered to life, sending a jolt of reaction crackling through him.

'You're beautiful.' His throat felt raw, his voice impeded. 'Every bit of you is perfect. Next to you, Aphrodite doesn't come close.'

'Not true,' she whispered, her voice a little shaky. 'There're definitely parts of me which aren't perfect. My leg...'

'Your leg is a part of you, and all of you is beautiful, inside and out.' He raised her hand to his mouth and kissed her fingers. 'And you taste deliciously of salt.'

'Not sweet, then?'

'So sweet, too.'

A tremor shook her.

'Loukas...'

'You're cold. Come, you need to get back to the house.'

'I'm not cold. I'll stay a little longer, if you want to go now.'

'And leave you on the beach, where you might go diving into the sea again?' He shook his head. 'Not happening.'

He stood up, took her hands and pulled her to her feet. Then he picked up the shirt she'd discarded on the sand, holding it out for her so she could push her arms into the sleeves. When she'd slipped her feet into her sandals, he took her hand and bent his head over it, turning it in his palm, tracing a little circle on the inside of her wrist with his thumb.

'Like I said, more beautiful than Aphrodite.'

Keeping her hand in his, he turned towards the path, but Sophia stood still. He looked back. 'I meant what I said. I refuse to leave you on the beach.'

'That's the first time I've seen you smile.'

He felt confused, as if he were in the middle of a different conversation. 'What do you mean?'

She tugged on his hand, bringing him closer to her. 'Then, when you mentioned Aphrodite. You smiled, and I haven't seen you smile before.'

'You haven't been paying attention, then. Anyway, have you been counting smiles?'

'No, but I have been paying attention. There's no doubt about it, although I'm willing to bet those are not laughter lines around your eyes.'

'So why did I smile now?'

'It was the notion of comparing me with Aphrodite. Obviously, you decided it was a silly idea.'

'No.' His expression had returned to its usual seriousness. 'I meant it.'

'Well, thank you. Since Aphrodite is the goddess of beauty and…love…that's a sweet compliment. But you should try smiling more often. It uses fewer muscles than frowning, and it made me feel…happy.'

He kept hold of her hand until they reached her door.

'Are you going back to work?'

She nodded. 'Yes, I must. Anna has left my fridge packed with delicious food. I'll eat later.'

'She and Stephanos have gone to a family party on Skiathos. They'll be away for a few days.'

'Anna was excited about it. She was looking forward to seeing her family. She—'

'Sophia, can I ask you something?'

A wariness came into her eyes. She tugged on her hand, but he held it fast.

'What?'

'On the beach, I thought you looked, just for a second…afraid?'

'Mmm.'

'I didn't mean to alarm you. I'm sorry. I don't want you to be afraid of me. Fear is corrosive. It erodes, slowly. It makes life narrow and restricted…'

Sophia's gaze was full of understanding, her luminous eyes soft with compassion. 'Yes, I know that, Loukas. We all deal with it in different ways.' She lifted her free hand and brushed her fingers across his cheek. 'But I wasn't afraid of you.'

'What was it, then?'

'I was afraid you wouldn't kiss me. And you didn't.'

She disengaged her hand from his and walked through the door, closing it behind her.

CHAPTER TEN

SOPHIA'S HAIR WAS stiff with salty seawater and there was sand between her toes. She turned the shower up to maximum and stepped under the spray, washing away the evidence of her swim.

It had been energising and therapeutic, but she felt a stab of guilt, remembering Loukas's discomfort on the beach.

He'd relaxed a little once she was out of the water, but not much.

She towelled herself dry and slipped into her silk bathrobe, wrapping it around herself and tying the sash firmly.

She'd thought he was going to kiss her. The straight and serious line of his mouth had softened a little when she'd stroked his tense hands, but he'd closed his eyes as if he didn't want to see her.

Only inches had separated his mouth from hers and she'd wanted to feel and taste him again with an ache she didn't recognise, although she knew that being in his arms, and feeling his sure hands on her body, would ease it.

But he hadn't kissed her. He'd urged her to get up and come back to the villa, where she'd eat another solitary meal, and have no excuse not to work.

If she hadn't sent him that email this morning, about the missing sculpture, she would never have known he was still on the island. She could have finished the assignment and returned to London without seeing him again and perhaps that was what he'd wanted.

Perhaps that would have been better than this. The memory of their shared kiss would fade eventually. It was being near him, absorbing his scent, watching emotion play over his features and seeing the flash of dark fire in his eyes that kept him at the centre of her thoughts.

She'd disrupted his solitude and he'd felt duty-bound to help her.

Had she contacted him just for the sake of it? Because she craved his attention?

He would have kissed her if he'd wanted to.

She took the chicken salad Anna had left for her onto the terrace and ate it while watching the last of the light drain from the sky. Her appetite, sharp after her swim, had faded.

He would have kissed her if he'd wanted to.

It had been the perfect opportunity, but he hadn't taken it.

She'd made a joke of it. How could she explain that the fear he'd seen in her eyes had been fear of herself? One touch of his lips would have sent her spinning over the edge, willingly abandoning the scruples she held about mixing work with pleasure.

She'd never considered herself a candidate for a quick fling, but now she wondered if that was what she wanted. Would it be a way to get this madness out of her system?

Had he been exercising restraint, or did he regard that kiss as a mistake? And was his compliment just to make her feel better about her leg?

She retreated inside and closed the French windows, leaving the shutters open so she could watch the darkness fall over the sea, and opened her laptop.

Her life, her *altered* life, was satisfying. The most excitement it provided was an artwork fetching a higher price than the estimate, or discovering something valuable, discarded in a disused basement. The adrenaline rush of performing before an audience was in the past, but she absolutely refused to allow herself to dwell on that loss. It had taken years to reach this point of acceptance, and she was happy with it now. Being a dancer had required exacting discipline and she'd used that practice to come to terms with the direction her injury had forced her to take.

Perhaps one day she'd reach a point where she could trust a man not to find her disfigurement off-putting but the future she'd originally envisaged, with a husband and family, had been re-shaped by the accident, as surely as her damaged leg and mangled bicycle.

But the coil of anticipation that had tightened in her abdomen, when Loukas's mouth had touched hers, threatened to upend all her hard work and careful planning and send her into a dangerous place of uncertainty and lack of control.

It was wickedly tempting.

Loukas did not expect to be able to sleep. It felt as if he'd hardly slept at all in the recent past and ever since Sophia's arrival it had been an elusive luxury.

He knew tonight would be no different.

She hadn't denied it had been fear he saw in her eyes, but he didn't believe her flippant response. She'd been covering up the fact that she'd felt out of her depth.

After he'd kissed her on the rock, she'd run from him, down the hillside, at a reckless and dangerous pace. Escaping from him on the beach wouldn't have been so easy, unless she'd gone back into the sea. She'd known he wouldn't follow her there.

Was he so intimidating? It was difficult to know. He didn't have anything by which to judge himself, but he found the idea that she might be afraid of him upsetting.

The little table in the courtyard where he'd eaten had felt inadequate. He could have suggested they eat together, but would that simply have added to her stress?

Back in the study, he removed his shoes, planted his feet on the desk and opened the drawer where he kept the bottle of whisky. Then he swore, slammed the drawer shut and left the room.

Memories crowded his head, which was already so full of 'what-ifs' he felt as if he was losing it altogether. As if pulled by an invisible thread of steel, he found himself standing in front of the portrait of Christos. Agonising regret joined the carousel in his brain as he made himself study his face. Christos looked back at him, his gaze faintly sardonic. There was an air of impatience about the picture, as if the subject had been anxious to get on with more important things than sitting in front of an artist. He'd been so brimful of energy, lust for life and...*love*.

Had he loved the girl who had been the cause of it all going so catastrophically wrong?

Loukas turned his back on the row of portraits and padded out of the sliding door onto the terrace. He skirted the pool and leaned on the balustrade. Far below, the sea gleamed like polished slate. He could hear the sinister heave and suck of the swells against the foot of the cliffs and the slap of small waves around the boulders on the beach.

He pulled a hand over his face, the ache of fatigue that was spreading through his body no match for the ache he felt for Sophia.

She'd been here less than a week, yet he felt as if he'd known her for ever.

He pushed himself upright and turned, at a loss. The darkest hours of the night still lay ahead, needing to be filled.

The pale oblong of light from Sophia's open window fell onto the terrace, unobstructed by the shutters. He thought he heard a sound, and listened more carefully, stilling his breath. It came again, and it sounded like a sob.

He crossed the terrace and tapped on her door.

It felt like an age before he heard a soft footstep.

'Who is that?'

Her voice was muffled. He was relieved she'd taken the precaution of identifying her visitor before opening the door.

'Loukas. Are you…?'

The door swung open, revealing the room in deep shadow. The only source of light came from the bedside lamp.

'Is something wrong?' Sophia was a dark silhouette, apart from the abrupt shimmer of her blonde hair as she took a step backwards, her hand on the edge of the door.

'No. Well, that is as long as you're okay? Are you still working? It's very late.'

'Yes, it's late, and yet you're up, too.'

'Can I come in?'

She hesitated, then opened the door wider, making space for him to step inside. The robe she wore was of navy-blue silk, tied at the waist, with long, loose sleeves and a plunging vee neck. She released the door, which swung closed on silent hinges, and her fingers fastened on the neck of the robe, pulling the edges towards each other, hiding her satiny skin.

He pulled his eyes away from her hands and raised them to her face. Beneath the slight tan she'd acquired on Alysos, her skin was paper-white. Her kissable mouth looked tender, the top lip slightly puffy.

Loukas narrowed his eyes. 'What happened to your mouth...?' Then he saw that her eyes were dark with emotion, and unnaturally bright. 'And your eyes?'

'Nothing.' She swiped the palm of her hand over her cheeks and sniffed. A tissue was balled up tightly in her other fist.

'You've been crying.'

'No, I haven't.'

Sophia turned her face away from Loukas, but he put his fingers under her chin and turned her head back towards the light.

'Yes, you have. What's wrong?'

She twisted out of his reach. 'Nothing's wrong. Now you know I'm okay, you can leave. Please.'

'Sophia, look at me. You're not okay.'

'No.' She shook her head. 'Please go.'

'I'm not going anywhere until you tell me why you've been crying.'

She crossed the room to the French doors. The moon had set and only starlight glimmered in the sky. She scrubbed at her eyes with the sodden tissue, with her back to him, and then tossed it towards the wastepaper basket. It missed and joined several others on the floor.

'Damn.'

'Here.' Loukas was behind her, holding out the box of tissues. 'Have a fresh one, but there're not many left.'

She pulled a tissue from the box and blew her nose. 'I'm sorry.'

'What for? Explain, and I can try to help.'

'How did you know I was awake?'

'I couldn't sleep.' He pushed his hands into his pockets. 'That's not strictly true. I didn't even try. And I heard you crying.'

'Next time I'll close the window.'

'There's going to be a next time? You said you don't cry.'

'Turns out sometimes I do.' There didn't seem any point in trying to keep up the pretence. 'Especially when you're around.'

'Would you care to tell me why?'

'Not really.' Sophia dropped her head. 'You don't have any shoes on.'

'Don't change the subject.' He opened the doors, stepped outside and pulled the shutters closed. 'And just so you're aware, sleep is probably not something I'm going to be able to do, so I'll wait. I've got all night.'

She raised her head and found herself staring into his eyes. His scorching scrutiny vapourised her flimsy layer of self-protection and she dropped her hands to her sides, admitting to herself that attempting to hide anything from him was probably futile.

And suddenly she no longer wanted to try. Her knees trembled and she backed towards the small sofa, folding herself onto it, pulling up her feet and tucking them under the hem of the robe.

Loukas sat on the ottoman at the foot of the bed and rested his elbows on his knees, his eyes on her face.

The silence stretched into minutes, but he didn't move. Finally, she drew in a deep breath and gave him a wobbly smile.

'It's a stupid thing. Not worth crying about, and not worth staying up all night to discuss...'

'Let me be the judge of that. For something to have upset you this much it must be worth discussing. Will it be keeping you up all night, worrying about it?' He straightened up and rested his hands on the ottoman, on either side of his hips.

She studied his face, catching her bottom lip

between her teeth. He looked exhausted. Stress showed in the line of his mouth and around his eyes.

Only a few hours ago she'd caressed the skin stretched over his knuckles, trying to get him to relax. She'd like to do that again, if she didn't think it would stress him even further. The sleeves of his linen shirt were rolled to the elbows, his corded forearms revealing the tension in the muscles of his arms. But his chest rose and fell evenly, in contrast to her shaky breathing.

She glanced towards her laptop, which stood open on the small table, but it had reverted to its screensaver mode. 'It's…'

His eyes had followed hers. 'Is it work?'

'No. It's something else…'

He turned his head, his eyes catching hers. 'So it's something personal. Who has upset you? I'll…' She saw his fists clench.

'Like I said, it's a stupid thing to cry over. And not personal, though I seem to be intent on making it about me instead of the people I've been asked to help. I hate being seen as a victim. It's not how I want to be defined.'

'No one who knows you, and the battles you've fought and won, could ever define you as anything other than brave and determined. And successful. You're not a victim. You're a conqueror.'

'If I thought that was true, I wouldn't be crying over it.'

'Like I said, let me be the judge. Tell me what "it" is, and I'll see what I think.'

'Okay, but be prepared to realise I'm behaving badly.' She smoothed the blue silk over her knees. 'I had an email from a charity. I've kept away from that kind of thing, since the accident. I didn't want to be identified with any of it. I wanted to make my own way, in privacy, to see what was possible and what wasn't. I suppose part of it was the fear of being seen to fail, in the glare of publicity.'

He nodded. 'I get that. Not everyone wants public sympathy. It can easily turn into judgement.'

'Anyway, at first the accident was news. Up-and-coming ballet star forced to retire, et cetera. I found it almost impossible to deal with. I was in pain. The person I had been no longer existed, in my mind, and somehow I had to find a new version of me. The press intrusion made that incredibly difficult. But as with all stories, a new one came along, and I was happy for mine to be forgotten.' Her voice cracked and she swallowed.

Loukas stood up and walked to the kitchenette, pulling a bottle of water from the fridge and filling a glass. He handed it to her and sat down on the opposite end of the sofa, sprawling against the cushions and stretching an arm along the back.

Sophia sipped the water. It was cool and soothing and the tense muscles in her jaw relaxed a little. 'Thank you.' She put the glass on the side table and linked her hands in front of her.

'What did this charity want from you? If it's money, I could...'

'No, nothing unreasonable.' She bent her head and her hair hid her face. 'They've asked if I'd be willing to address their annual conference. They want me to talk about what it was like to lose the career I loved, the thing I was passionate about above all else, and how I managed to overcome what they term "the difficulty" and retrain to become something else.'

'They want you to talk to a room full of people about the thing you never talk about to anyone.'

'Well, yes. You've managed to distil that neatly into one sentence.'

His fingers drummed on the back of the sofa. 'Say no.'

'But that would be so selfish. It would be making it all about me. What about the people who need help, or perhaps need to be inspired to change how they feel about themselves?'

'It *is* about you. It's about not doing something that might upset your mental health. You've told me how hard it's been to get to where you are now. You need to make sure you stay strong enough to maintain what you've achieved.'

'I don't think refusing this request would help me to stay strong. I think it would be weak.'

'That doesn't seem like a good enough reason to do it. Or why you're so upset.'

Her throat ached with more tears, and she grabbed the glass of water and swallowed two mouthfuls. 'Except for the other day, I haven't cried for…for ever. But talking to you about the accident brought everything back to the surface. I've been struggling to find some sort of equilibrium over the past few days. I hadn't had a flashback for a long time…'

'And you've had them again?'

She nodded. 'And a nightmare. It makes me afraid to sleep. The swim this afternoon was so therapeutic. I really felt better, but then this email came and I…'

His hand dropped from the back of the sofa to rest on her shoulder, massaging it with a light touch. 'And you're back to square one.'

She tipped her head to the side for a moment, brushing her cheek against his fingers. 'A week ago, I wouldn't have hesitated. I'd have said "yes" without a second thought. I was confident. I had no reason to think I wouldn't be able to do it.'

'And that was before you talked about it, to me. Or anyone.'

'Yes. I'm not upset that they asked. It's a perfectly natural request and they probably see me as an excellent example of what they're trying to promote. I'm upset because I've discovered how fragile and…unstable…my emotions really are, when I believed something else. I've lost confidence. I can't...*trust*...myself, and that's something that has been fundamental to the way I've learned to live my life. I've never had trust in anyone—my parents were dead and my grandparents... I could never trust them with my emotions because they refused to talk to me about my parents, and their loss was what I wanted to talk about most of all.' She lifted her shoulders. 'I have to trust myself. I don't want to become a self-centred victim.'

Loukas's hand slid off her shoulder and down her arm and closed around her fingers. 'The fact that you're having this argument with yourself proves you're nothing of the sort, Sophia. If you were self-centred, you'd have refused the request at once, without questioning your motives. Instead of that, you've worried yourself into a state of confusion and doubt.' His thumb stroked across the pulse at her wrist and her heart thumped against her ribs. 'Is there anything you'd like? A drink?'

'No, thank you. I just want to try to clear my head and think about it tomorrow, by which time I hope I'll feel back in control.' She looked across at him and smiled. 'You've helped, just by being here.'

'I'm glad I didn't leave when you asked me to.'

'I'm glad, too.'

'If you'd like me to go now, I will.'

She looked down at their linked hands. 'No. I'd like you to stay.'

His fingers tightened around hers. 'Are you sure?' His voice was quiet.

When she lifted her eyes to his she saw a depth of emotion in them that made her heart turn over. 'Yes,' she murmured. 'I'm very sure.'

'Sophia.'

He tugged her towards him. His hand traced a path up her arm, back to her shoulder, and then on, to the back of her head. She felt him spike his fingers into her hair and then hold her steady. His other hand rested on her waist and her body leapt in response to the light pressure of it. The dark flame in his eyes told her he'd felt it, too. That chemistry, volatile and dangerous, hissed between them, generating white-hot heat that settled in her abdomen, melting and pouring into her veins to reach every part of her.

'Loukas…'

His mouth was a whisper from hers. 'Yes, *agape mou*.'

His lips, warm and firm, brushed her mouth, tasting and testing her response. She twisted, to bring her body closer to the hard muscles of his chest, placing her hands on his shoulders and feeling the male strength of him beneath her palms and questing fingers. The erotic slide of his tongue against hers made her arch towards him, wanting more contact with him, and then her head dropped back against the sofa cushions as his mouth left hers to travel over her throat, to the exquisite spot where the curve of her shoulder began.

He kissed the pulse beating frantically there, and Sophia, taking her turn, pushed her fingers into his hair and pulled him down to her. She felt his hand move between them and tug at the sash of the robe and her own hand drifted down to rest over his.

He raised his head, his molten gaze melting her again. 'Do you want to stop?' His voice sounded thick and hoarse, evidence of his struggle to keep it even.

Her mind was spinning away from her, all her anxiety and uncertainty dissolving in the heat of this moment. Coherent thought became impossible as emotion and desire swept through her, but there was one thing she was certain about, on a level of her consciousness that floated above all reason or argument.

'No,' she whispered. She lifted her hand and locked it onto the front of his shirt. 'I don't want to stop. And I don't want to rip any more buttons off any more of your shirts.'

He smiled against her mouth. 'You could try undoing them...'

Knowing he'd smiled for her, she felt pleasure, hot and urgent, race through her. 'You smiled, again. It's made my hands shake.' But her fingers threaded through his hair, fluttered across his cheekbone and stroked across his lips. A muscle in his jaw clenched as she trailed them over his throat, to the neck of his shirt.

She managed two buttons before she slipped her hand under the supple linen, raking her nails lightly through the mist of dark hair that covered his chest. She felt his body tense, the muscles in his shoulders bulge, and then he muttered something in Greek and his mouth swooped onto hers. There was nothing in this kiss to remind her of his earlier gentleness. His mouth demanded everything, and she gave it all, willingly, matching the stroke of his tongue with answering thrusts of her own, and catching his bottom lip between her teeth when he held her head between his hands and tipped her face up towards his.

Then her breath stuttered in her chest as his capable hand slid over her breast, finding the hardened nipple through the slide of the silk.

'Loukas… I…'

He stood, in one fluid movement, scooping her against his chest, and strode to the bed, lying down with her in his arms, ripping the sash from the robe and parting it.

In a reflexive movement, Sophia tried to cover her thigh, but he circled her wrists with his fingers and eased her hands away.

His voice was rough. 'Don't hide from me, Sophia.' His gaze left her face to travel slowly over her body, leaving a trail of heat and desire on her sensitised skin. 'You're so beautiful. Every part of you is exquisite.' He rested his fingers lightly on her scarred thigh. She flinched.

'Does it hurt you?' Concern clouded his eyes and he lifted his hand.

'No. It doesn't hurt. But the idea of you seeing it scares me.'

'Don't be afraid. It doesn't shock me.' He smoothed the silk robe back over the damaged skin. 'But if you're more comfortable covering it up, that's okay. You're in control.'

She smiled. 'If this is control…'

'I don't want to do anything that makes you uneasy.' He let go of her wrists and her hands moved to his shoulders, feeling his powerful muscles flex. 'I'll be guided by you.'

His dark eyes, burning with sincerity, held hers. She slid a hand along the silk edge of the robe, easing it away from her body. Loukas took his weight on his forearms and followed the movement.

'If you're sure you want to see it…'

'I want to see all of you, Sophia, even this. I know you don't agree with me.' He rested his forehead against hers. 'But this has made you what you are, and it is beautiful.'

CHAPTER ELEVEN

LOUKAS WOKE WITH Sophia curled into his side. One hand was tucked under her cheek, the other rested on his chest. Pale early morning light was beginning to seep through the shutters and the bedside lamp still cast a pool of light onto the nightstand.

This was unknown territory for him. He did not spend the night in a woman's bed or invite one to his. Not ever. But finding Sophia's warm body next to his felt astonishingly right. They'd both slept deeply. He was refreshed and relaxed for the first time in what felt like years.

Heated, raw passion had been followed by slow exploration and tender lovemaking. The stirring of fresh desire tightened his body as he remembered. He didn't want to wake her, but he was ready to take her in his arms, all over again.

He lifted her hand from his chest and turned on his side, folding it in both of his, careful not to disturb her but needing to study her pure profile. Colour flushed her cheek and her lips and the sweep of her eyelashes shadowed her creamy skin. A light sprinkling of freckles, probably the product of the Greek sun, dusted her nose. She looked tranquil and he hoped she would wake feeling as relaxed as he did.

How could he express to her the depth of emotion that had stirred in him at the courage she'd shown last night? The way she'd willingly revealed her injury? Her trust felt like a fragile gift, which he would do his utmost to deserve. He vowed to himself that she would never have a reason to regret entrusting something so precious to him.

Sophia stirred in her sleep, shuffling closer to him, and the cotton sheet covering both of them slipped from her shoulder. Loukas lifted it to drape it back over the creamy curve of her breast, with its rosebud tip that had proved so exquisitely sensitive to the attention of his fingers and mouth.

The light had strengthened, sunlight now lying in bright bars across the floor, where it had found its way past the slats in the shutters. There was no need to wake her yet. They were alone on the island. They could stay in bed all day, if they chose.

Gently he disentangled his legs from hers and inched himself away from her, towards the edge of the bed. She muttered something in her sleep and drew in a deep breath. He dropped a kiss on her temple. 'I'll make us coffee, sweetheart,' he whispered as she settled back into sleep.

As he crossed the terrace to the sliding glass doors, he realised they'd stood open all night. All responsible thought had been driven from his mind by the feel of Sophia's lithe body against his hard thighs and chest. Her softness and willingness had driven him wild with desire, but he'd done his best to rein it in, to be gentle and careful with her.

She hadn't made that easy. The sound of his name on her lips, her urgent responses to his touch, had been off-the-scale sensual. The way she'd arched into him had driven him to the very edge of self-control, and, eventually, over it.

In the aftermath of their lovemaking, he'd asked her to stay longer so they could explore this extraordinary chemistry that had brought them together, enjoy it while they could, without commitment, where nobody would discover them. He was very afraid she'd refuse.

Carrying two mugs of coffee, he padded across the floor and stood looking down at her, savouring these moments before she woke and gave him her answer. She still slept, her cheek on her folded arm, her other arm thrown above her head, the spun gold of her hair spread across the pillow. His stomach clenched with desire.

He slipped into the bed beside her and she murmured and stirred. He pulled the rumpled linen over his legs and hips and leaned into the pillows, then he gathered her against him, tracing a finger over her cheek and settling her into his arms.

She shifted and slid a hand onto his chest. 'Loukas?'

He dropped a kiss on the top of her head. 'You were expecting someone else?'

Her eyelids fluttered open, and her mouth curved in that smile that tugged at his heart and stalled his thoughts.

Her hand fluttered across his ribs, and he dropped his own over it, entwining his fingers with hers. 'Any lower, and I won't be responsible for what happens next.'

'Promise?' She pressed her cheek into his shoulder. 'We left responsibility behind us, somewhere on the floor, last night. I think it's overrated.'

'I made coffee...'

'I've got you. You're dark and intense. You make my heart beat faster than any amount of caffeine and you kept me awake...for hours.'

'You're a temptress.'

'Mmm. Like Peitho. She was the goddess of temptation, and Aphrodite's companion.'

'I can't resist you.'

'I don't want you to try.'

Sophia sat at her desk and stared out of the window. She'd started work late and had achieved precisely nothing in the past two hours. Concentration was impossible. Her wayward mind strayed constantly to images of Loukas in her bed, and to the question he'd asked her last night, and again this morning.

Could she stay longer? *Should* she?

In London, Sean was agitating for her to return as quickly as possible to play a role in organising the sale. He'd put an impressive team together, but he wanted her to be a part of it. She'd seen the collection. He valued her judgement. According to him, she had to get herself back before the world ended.

But she knew she could spin this out for a few more days and no one would ever suspect it wasn't necessary.

If the extra days happened to be a weekend, would that make it okay? She'd already mentioned to Loukas that she hoped to take a few days' holiday at the end of the assignment. What if she took them, and spent them with him?

She'd failed to keep her work separate from her personal life. But if she stayed after she'd finished the job, she'd technically no longer be working for him. Would that make it better?

Since her injury, she hadn't had a personal life.

Had the time come to indulge in a fling? Was that what Loukas intended? He'd told her he never formed lasting relationships and she'd be no different. Could she cope with leaving him behind, knowing it was over? That by next week he'd be in New York or Hong Kong, possibly with some sophisticated woman who had no qualms about his lifestyle?

She didn't think she could. What she was beginning to feel for him already went deeper than anything she'd experienced before. Should she finish it now and walk away while she still could, with her heart secretly broken but her head held high?

Or should she allow herself these few days of intense happiness and fulfilment, knowing she was submitting herself to a lifetime of missing him, after they'd parted?

Questions flew at her from all directions.

Loukas knew she'd be returning to London in a few days' time, bringing a finite end to whatever this was between them. There'd be no difference between her and any other woman in his life. Why would there be? His lovemaking was skilled and tender, the emotions he expressed heartfelt, but in all the words they'd whispered to each other, neither of them had hinted at this idyll lasting beyond her departure.

All she knew was that she wanted to be with him, in his arms, in his bed.

She flipped the file on her desk shut and stood up.

CHAPTER TWELVE

AFTER LOSING THE thread of his concentration on a third business call, Loukas told his PA in Athens he was unavailable for the rest of the day.

How could he discuss the commissioning of a new container vessel when all he was able to think about was the honey-coloured sunlight gilding Sophia's body, and the soft words she'd whispered to him in the early-morning light?

He carried the brown envelope she had given him out to the table on the shady terrace, ran a finger under the seal and tipped out the contents.

A collection of loose photographs slithered onto the table, along with a brightly coloured pouch bearing the logo and address of a photographic shop on Skiathos. Gold gleamed in a shaft of sunlight as a fine chain sifted through his fingers. He picked up the heart-shaped locket, encrusted with seed pearls, he'd last seen around the neck of Christos's grandmother, in the portrait on the drawing room wall. But when he examined it more closely, he saw that half of it was missing.

He slipped it into his shirt pocket, pulled out his glasses and bent over the photographs.

'Loukas?'

Sophia stood in the doorway. He pulled off his spectacles and his breath caught, as he thought it would every time he saw her. She wore the pale blue sundress she'd put on earlier. Her feet were bare and her bright hair was loose around her shoulders. Loukas stood and stretched out a hand.

'Not working?'

She walked towards him, and he folded her into his arms.

'The thought of you kept obstructing a billion-dollar deal. I've handed it over to someone else.'

'Says the man who travels the world to make sure his business is running smoothly.'

He pressed his mouth to the top of her head.

'Mmm. Rose and...?'

'Geranium. It's the shampoo.'

He lifted a hand from where it rested on her shoulder blades and ran his fingers through her hair.

'You're not working, either. Or have you come up against another problem?'

'You're my problem. I can't concentrate either. At least, not on artists beginning with V, even though I think I have just seen a small oil by Van Gogh.'

'Forget him for a while and come and look at what was in the envelope.'

The colours of the prints had faded, and most of them seemed to have been taken on Alysos, around the harbour, on the terrace where they now sat, or on the beach.

'I think they're a record of a number of years.' Sophia picked up one of the photographs. 'If you compare them, you can see how this girl has grown up. She looks about ten here.' She tapped another picture. 'But here she looks more sophisticated. Her hair is no longer in plaits—it's loose.'

Loukas nodded. 'I think this is Christos as a teenager. And in this one he's older. He has that self-confident look I remember. He almost always got what he wanted.'

'Is this you? As a child?' Sophia handed a print to Loukas.

'Mmm.' He dropped the photograph and opened the flap of the remaining envelope, extracting a few colour prints. They were clearer, the colours sharper. 'Here I am, a few years older.' The image was of a small boy, staring unsmiling at the camera. Christos's arm was draped around his shoulders, but his eyes were fixed on the young woman next to him, who'd grown up into a pale, ethereal blonde. He wished he could remember her name.

He dropped the photo and straightened up, unwelcome memories swooping down on him.

'What's wrong?' Sophia's eyes were concerned.

'Just memories.'

'Not good ones.'

'Not of that year. No.'

Her hand closed over his and he turned his palm and interlaced his fingers with hers. She bent her head over the pictures, scooping her hair up in one hand and holding it out of the way.

'It's weird. It almost feels to me as if there's something familiar about that picture, but I can't work out what it is.'

Loukas reached for another, which had fallen upside down from the envelope, and noticed faded writing on the white backing. He angled it to the light.

'"The face that launched a thousand ships",' he read, out loud.

'Helen,' said Sophia.

He turned the print over and heard her small gasp. He looked from the image in his hand, to her face and then back to the picture. His mind froze and then roared into overdrive.

'Helen of Troy,' he said, frowning. 'But...'

'Helen was my mother's name.' There was a tremor in Sophia's voice. 'And she...the person in that picture...'

'Looks exactly like you.' He replaced the print on the table, keeping his eyes on Sophia. The colour had drained from her cheeks, her wide mouth opened slightly in shock.

'No!' The word was almost strangled in her throat. 'It can't be. How could it be? It's...impossible.' Her hands flew to her mouth, and she shook

her head, her hair swinging across her face. 'Tell
me it's not, Loukas.'

'I can't tell you, Sophia, because I don't know.'

Sophia shuffled the pictures in front of her
with shaking hands. 'But look, Loukas, at this
one. This is the one that looked familiar. And it's
because of...*them*.'

He frowned, looking at where her forefinger
stabbed the image. 'They're her parents.'

'Loukas, they're my *grandparents*.' Her expression was stricken. 'I've never seen a picture
of my mother, but I remember my grandparents.'
She leapt up, toppling the chair over behind her.
'How can this be true?' She snatched up the picture again, staring at it. 'Why were they here?
Every year?'

Her voice broke on a sob, and then she took a
deep, shuddering breath. She swiped the heel of
her hand across her cheeks and swallowed hard.
'Okay.' She shook her head. 'There must be some
other explanation. That can't...she can't be...my
mother.'

Her eyes appealed to him for help, but he was
at a loss as to how to offer her comfort. His mind
raced as he tried to delve into those distant memories that he preferred to keep locked up. Looking back, that final summer on Alysos felt filled
with darkness and trepidation but he knew he
was colouring it with his own memories of how
it had ended.

He stood and took Sophia's hands in his, pulling her towards him. 'Try to breathe, sweetheart. We'll work this out. Perhaps this is just an incredible coincidence—someone who looks very like you.'

'Loukas, those *are* my grandparents. Why would they have someone with them who looks like me but *wasn't* my mother?'

He shook his head. 'I don't know, but we'll explore all the possibilities. And I have an idea of how we can begin.'

Hope lit her features. 'Now? Can we do it now?'

He nodded. 'Will you be all right here on your own for a few minutes? I'll be right back.'

Loukas carried a large, leather-bound book across the terrace. The edges were marbled, and the word 'Visitors' was stamped in gold leaf on the cover.

'This was in Christos's desk. It goes back decades. I remember,' he said, placing the book on the desk and righting the unturned chair, 'the ceremony of visitors always having to write in it.' His hands on her shoulders, he guided Sophia into the chair and then turned his attention to the book. He flipped through the thick cream pages, to the last few entries, running his index finger down the list of names.

'There!' Sophia whispered as his finger stopped. 'Alan, Marjorie and Helen Shaw.' She raised her eyes to his. 'That's all the proof we need, isn't it?'

Loukas nodded. 'The date is the day before… they left, that year. That last year.'

Sophia stood up, biting her lip. He took her hand. 'Sit down, Sophia. We can talk about this. I'll make some coffee…' But she tugged her fingers away and took a step backwards, shaking her head. 'No. I c-can't. Not now. I need to think about this, on my own. I'm…shocked. I…'

'Of course.' He stood and she took another step away from him. 'Do you need anything? Let me…'

'No, thank you. I'll…maybe I'll see you later.'

He nodded. 'I'm here, when you want to talk.'

He watched her walk away, his heart aching. He wanted to hold her, tell her it was all okay, that this didn't change anything, but he couldn't do that because he knew it did. It changed everything, and, despite her distress, he didn't think Sophia had realised the full implication of what they'd discovered, yet.

The photographs were spread out over the table and he gathered them together, keeping the close-up of Helen aside. Whatever happened, Sophia must have that one.

One last print had become stuck in the envelope, and he pulled it out, seeing it had a note fixed to it with a rusty paperclip. It was a picture of the Aphrodite.

He read the note.

She reminds me of H. I'll put her where I can see her every day.

It was hours later when Sophia slid off her bed and headed for the bathroom. She splashed cold water on her face and brushed her hair, avoiding her reflection in the mirror. She didn't need confirmation of how awful she looked.

The facts that had stared up at her from those photographs could not be twisted in any way that would lead to a different conclusion. Panic, which she'd first experienced after her accident, threatened to derail her completely. She kept a tight lid on it, using breathing techniques and trying to think logically.

There were questions she had to ask Loukas, and they couldn't wait.

She found him on the terrace, leaning on the balustrade. He turned when he heard her, and came towards her. His expression was guarded, and he made no move to touch her.

The photos had gone from the table, but a single white envelope lay there, with her name on it. He nodded towards it.

'That's for you. It's the picture of Helen—your mother. You must keep it.'

She nodded. 'Thank you.'

They sat opposite each other, and she gripped her hands together in her lap, catching her bottom lip between her teeth.

'Sophia—'

'No. Please don't say anything. I need to ask you...'

'I'll try to help, if I can.'

'I need to ask...was Christos my father?'

His silence seemed to stretch into minutes. Then he folded his arms on the table and nodded. 'I think he was.'

'Why? Why do you think so?'

She saw his chest expand as he sucked in a deep breath.

'Because...of the way they were together, that summer. If you look at the pictures, in every one he's not looking at the camera, he's looking at her. And his expression gives his feelings away. So does hers.'

'But they could have just fancied each other. She might have had another boyfriend back in England. Just because they're looking at each other, it doesn't mean...'

He held up a hand. 'It's not just that. Christos used to see them on trips to London, and at art fairs in Europe. I know, because Helen used to send gifts back for me. I still have the toy soldiers...' He paused. 'And it's also because of what I saw.'

'I know talking about Christos is difficult for you.' Sophia pulled a tissue from her pocket, keeping it bunched in her fist. 'And I know you never talk about how he died. But if you really believe he was my father, I need to know.'

Loukas stood. 'Come with me. I want to show you something.' He walked away, into the drawing room. When Sophia caught up with him he was standing in front of the portrait of Christos's grandmother. He took out his phone and switched on the torch facility, focussing it on the picture. 'Do you see that?'

Sophia leaned towards the picture. The artist had painted a tiny, dark, heart-shaped mark on the creamy skin of the woman's left breast, close to the lace that edged the deep neckline of her gown.

She nodded. 'It looks like a birthmark. It looks...'

'You have exactly the same mark, in the same place. I noticed it last night, but I didn't stop to think about it. We were...' He looked away and Sophia saw a spasm of emotion cross his face. 'It wasn't until today, after we'd seen those pictures, that I thought about it again. It's a mark many of the Georgiou women have.'

Her hand went to her left breast. 'It could just be nothing. It's so small. I could have a DNA test...'

'It might be difficult to find anyone to test against. Christos had no living relatives.'

They returned to the terrace and faced each other across the table. Sophia ached for the comfort of his touch, but he sat upright, arms folded rigidly across his chest.

'When you spoke of what you saw, I thought you were talking about Christos and Helen.'

'Before I talk about that, we need to talk about us.' Then he did lean forward and reach out to take her hands. 'Because you realise this changes everything, for both of us, don't you?'

Sophia lifted her shoulders, not sure what he meant. 'In a way, yes. If Christos was my father, it means that, on one day, I've seen a picture of my mother and discovered the identity of my father.'

'It means, if you can prove it, you are his heir. You could challenge the will. You could be the owner of Alysos, and all the art.'

She stared at him, an ice-cold wave of shock sweeping through her. 'No,' she whispered, 'I don't want that.'

'Why? It would be liberating for you. If you sell it, you'd have your own fortune, to do with as you please.'

'That is not the life I want. I like the life I've made for myself. I'm in control of it. I don't want to change it.'

'And what if I decide to share this information with my lawyers? It would be a way of getting rid of Alysos and the collection without having to go through the process of the public auction, the worry of having the press find me here, bringing up the story of Christos again.'

'I've promised you that won't happen. Marshalls is keeping everything under wraps until the art has been shipped out. And anyway, what is the story you're worried about? It was all a long time ago. People lose interest. I know that from personal experience.'

Sophia felt a space growing between them, which she desperately needed to close. Loukas looked distant, severe. Unreachable. The panic she'd been suppressing all afternoon clawed at her.

'Loukas...'

He let go of her hands and sat back, retreating even further from her.

'We can't do this any more, Sophia. Not now. Surely you can see that?'

'But we don't need to tell anyone. Why can't we keep it a secret? And anyway, it's only until I leave.'

'I think Christos would have wanted you to inherit his fortune, if he'd known about you. Don't you?'

She stared at him. His eyes were sombre. 'I don't know. And you don't, either, Loukas. Perhaps he would have shared it between us.'

'He only made me his heir because he felt responsible for the deaths of my parents and he had no relatives. He knew I didn't need his inheritance. Whereas you...' He returned her steady gaze. 'It would be life-changing for you. When you've had time to get used to the idea you might feel differently. This is overwhelming for you.

You need to consider it carefully before making any decisions.'

Sophia felt a tide of despair rising in her chest. A few short hours ago she'd been floating on a cloud of joy but it had all turned to ashes. How had it happened?

'My life has already changed beyond recognition, Loukas. What we've shared has changed me.'

He reached across the table and brushed his knuckles along her jaw. 'I know,' he said quietly, 'and this has been a time I will remember and cherish and keep in my heart, but I cannot risk it becoming public knowledge and possibly jeopardising any claim you might make. I could be seen as trying to coerce you into refusing the inheritance.'

'And if I refuse to make a claim? Even after considering it? What then?'

'Integrity dictates that I must tell my lawyers what we've discovered. Christos would have loved you, Sophia. He would have wanted to care for you.'

'If Christos was my father I would have loved him, too. I need to know what happened to him,' she whispered.

Loukas's heart cracked at the sight of the determined, fragile figure opposite him. He wanted to reach out and take her hands, pull her into his arms, but he tucked his clenched fists into his armpits and looked away from her pinched face, over her shoulder towards the olive grove. He took a breath.

'Okay. If you're sure you want this now.'

'I'm sure.'

'It was the summer when I was eight. I...'

'That was the summer Christos died, wasn't it?'

'It was. That envelope of the newest photos is dated the previous day. Your grandparents and Helen had been here for about a week, I think. Helen had just had her birthday party. One of those photos is of the cake. It has "twenty-four" on it, in pale pink sugar roses. I think Christos' parents met Alan at an antiques fair in London ten years before that and invited him to Alysos with his wife and daughter. That must have been when Christos and Helen first met. Looking at the photos, celebrating Helen's birthday on the island became an annual tradition.'

Loukas leaned forwards, freeing his hands and resting his folded arms on the table. 'But that year felt different. Christos and Helen were inseparable and I sensed tension between them and her parents. I was jealous because they seemed to have little time for me.' He pulled his hands across his face, massaging his eyes. 'Helen was very beautiful. But delicate.'

Sophia nodded. 'One of the few things I know

about my mother was that a childhood illness had damaged her heart. She'd been told never to have children, but she insisted on having me. I've always felt so guilty...'

'Ah. I understand. Christos and your grandfather had an argument. There was shouting, which frightened me. They were supposed to leave the following day. That night, I heard Christos leave the house. I felt anxious so I followed him.'

'What happened, Loukas?' Her words were barely a whisper.

'He and Helen met, on the cliff above the beach. They were lying on the grass, and I thought he was hurting her. I knew I shouldn't be there, but I was afraid to move in case they saw me. But then your grandfather found them. He was in a rage. He pulled Helen away. She was crying, screaming at her father, trying to cover herself. Then he let her go and turned back Christos. They began to argue again.'

'Can you remember what they said?'

'No. I...ran away, back to the villa. I was terrified.'

Her face was ghostly white and her breath came in shallow gasps. 'What happened?'

'The following morning Stephanos found Christos's body at the foot of the cliff. Your grandparents' cruiser had gone, but they were always due to leave early that morning. The death was treated as an accident, or suicide. There was alcohol in his system.'

'Did you tell anyone about the argument?'

'The police came from Skiathos to investigate.' He bit his lip, taking a few breaths before continuing. 'I told them I hadn't seen or heard anything. That I'd been in my bed all night, which is where Stephanos and Anna found me in the morning, when they came to tell me Christos was dead.'

'Why didn't you tell them what you'd seen?'

He shook his head. 'I was eight. I was terrified about what would happen to me. And nothing I said would bring Christos back.'

Quiet settled over them. Sophia tried to imagine being eight years old and witnessing something so frightening. Her childhood had been lonely, but she hadn't been traumatised. She'd just been unloved and blamed for the death of her mother. The accident had tested her strength and determination to the limit, but she'd fought that battle, and won.

Loukas lived with the memory of loss and horror, every day of his life. She understood now why he felt burdened by his inheritance from Christos. The island held bitter, terrifying memories for him, from losing his parents and almost drowning, to the death of his beloved godfather. He'd lost all the people he loved.

She looked into his dark eyes, seeing pain, but also relief.

'I'll understand…' he heaved in a breath '…if you want to leave. This is shocking news for you, and…'

'Yes,' she said, nodding slightly. 'It is and I probably should leave. But I must finish what I've been sent to do, even if you decide to cancel the sale. Please give me time to complete the catalogue, before you do anything.'

He was quiet for a long time until, finally, he nodded. 'Okay. I can do that. When do you think you'll finish?'

'I need three more days.'

'Friday, then.'

He stood up and walked around to stand behind her. She felt his strong hands on her shoulders and breathed in his scent as he bent over her. She turned her face up to look at him and he kissed her, hard, on the mouth. Then he straightened up and walked away.

It felt like a goodbye in everything but words.

Sophia felt like a fundamentally different person. The information about her parents, longed for over so many years, seemed unreal, but the evidence of her grandparents' and mothers' supposed travels in the Aegean, in the well-used guidebook, had suddenly gained credibility. There was a possibility that she could be an heiress. Confusion made her rub her eyes, her thoughts tripping over one another.

Loukas had said he'd give her time to think it through, but she couldn't do this on her own. The only person she wanted to discuss it with, the only person she *could* discuss it with, was him, but he had distanced himself. Had he said she should leave on Friday? Or was Friday the day by which she had to decide what she wanted to do?

And if she refused to claim the inheritance, could he make her? Could anyone?

Would he be harsh enough to ignore what she wanted? She realised, with a pain that stabbed at her heart, that she didn't know.

CHAPTER THIRTEEN

HE'D AVOIDED HER for two days. He'd retreated behind the locked door of his apartment to make sure they didn't meet. The thought of seeing her and not being able to touch her, hold her, kiss her, was unbearable. The ache of missing her was a constant reminder of all he'd lost.

These feelings, which had taken hold of him in a grip that he couldn't break, terrified him. They were what he'd guarded against for as long as he could remember, because they had the power to destroy him. He'd lost his parents and Christos, and he was never going to allow himself to care about losing another soul. It hurt too much. It made you lose control of your life. He kept his heart protected, guarded it carefully. It wasn't available for breaking, again.

He depended on and trusted only himself, but suddenly those feelings made him want to share things with Sophia. It felt like a massive betrayal, of himself and of his lifestyle.

More than once, he had hovered his finger

over his lawyer's name on his phone, wanting to change things. If he could start the process of making Sophia the heir to Christos's fortune, at least he'd make something happen although the satisfaction would be bleak. As soon as this information became known by anyone other than the two of them, he'd have lost control of it. Any relationship between them would have to be denied.

Was that what they had? A relationship? It wasn't what he wanted, but what about Sophia? She'd been changed, she said. Did that mean she wanted more from him? More than he could ever promise? He felt panic clawing at him at the thought of it.

He'd walked away from her and he had to stay away from her, to protect her and to protect himself.

He'd made a promise and he must keep it. Contacting his legal team on Monday would be soon enough.

Friday, when she'd said she'd have finished the assignment, crept closer, and the dread of her leaving loomed like a dark shadow. Even if he avoided seeing her, knowing she was still there kept the darkness that threatened to overwhelm him at bay.

Then, on Thursday afternoon, she sent him an email.

There is something I need to discuss with you.

The ten minutes he waited to reply felt like hours. Had she changed her mind about the inheritance? Could he trust himself to see her? He finally tapped into his phone.

I'll come to your office.

He stopped in the open doorway, waiting for Sophia to register his presence. She wore the blue sundress that matched her eyes. Her hair was pulled into a ponytail and he flexed his fingers, longing to ease it free of the restraining band and feel its silkiness tumble over his hands. He took a steadying breath, and she turned, and, even though he was prepared for it, the collision of their eyes sent a shockwave rippling through him.

'This is hell.' The words were out of his mouth before he could stop them. 'I don't know if I can do it.'

'I'm sorry. There's a problem. But I'll email you, if it's easier…' Her voice caught and he saw her swallow.

'I haven't slept since we made love. I need you. But, Sophia, I can't… Is this about the will?'

She shook her head. 'No. It's something else, but…' He saw her fingers curl inwards, nails digging into her palms, and her teeth close over her trembling bottom lip. 'Yes,' she said. 'It is hell. I can't sleep. I…miss you.' Her eyes on his were steady and the depth of need he saw in them stalled his breath.

'I don't know why you're doing this. If it's because you think I want more from you, please… listen to me. Because I don't. That is, I know you don't do relationships. I know once I leave, tomorrow, this will be over. But I think what we have is special and so let us have it until tomorrow. I promise no one else will ever know and you need never hear from me again, if you don't want to.' She dropped her head, as if she didn't want to see him reject her. 'Make love to me, Loukas. Just tonight.'

Then she was in his arms. He locked her against his length, obliterating any space between them, cupping the back of her head and easing her hair out of its restraint. His heart thundered in a drumbeat against his ribs. As he buried his face in her hair the relief that rolled over him was almost too much to bear.

She looked up at him and her luminous eyes shone with desire as his mouth hovered over hers, brushing her lips.

'Sophia.' He groaned her name. 'Whatever this is between us is too strong to resist. I can't fight it any more.'

'I can't either,' she whispered. 'I don't want to.'

He swept her up, holding her against his chest, and strode along the passage towards his apartment, kicking the door shut behind them. In his bedroom he let her slide down his body until her toes touched the floor. He took her face between his hands and kissed her, savouring her taste and scent, before the passion, which he was trying to hold in check, broke free and stole any ability he might still have to take this slowly.

'You wanted to discuss something,' he said, dragging his mouth from hers with a supreme effort.

'It can wait. I can't.'

'Stay,' he whispered into her mouth. 'Please stay. Until Monday.'

By the morning there were nine more emails in Sophia's inbox, written in the short, staccato sentences that meant Sean was in a state of high excitement.

She read them, but her ability to concentrate was in shreds, memories of their night of lovemaking a constant obstruction to rational thought. Yesterday she'd been going to discuss this with Loukas. It had felt important then.

Leaving her office, she went in search of him. She could have stayed and formulated a response to Sean's over-the-top messages, but she and Loukas had been apart for two hours and memories of the night were not enough to satisfy her hunger for him.

She found him in the olive grove. He held out his arms and his beautiful mouth curved in the smile that made her heart turn over. He bent his head to kiss her, then spun her round, pulling her against him and wrapping her in an embrace.

'The colour of the sky is a reflection of your eyes.'

She tipped her head back against his chest. 'The sky has the stronger claim. It was there first.'

He bent his head. 'Mmm. That was just an excuse to make you look up so I could kiss you.'

He pulled her down onto the rough grass under one of the twisted olives and settled her into the space between his thighs. She leaned against him, feeling the hard planes of his body supporting her, and she filled her lungs, savouring his male scent. He swept her hair aside with one hand and pressed his lips to the nape of her neck.

'I came to tell you something but I'm in danger of forgetting what it was.'

'I need you. Can't you take a break?'

She smiled, enjoying the warmth of his body against her and the sunshine on her face.

'I could stay here all day, but then I'd have to work tonight. I...lost time yesterday. Are you okay with that?'

'No.' His voice was rough. 'I'm not.'

'Then...' She tried to straighten up, but he held her anchored between his thighs, his fingers combing her hair off her forehead.

'Tell me what you came to say, then you can forget about work for a while and soak up the sun. You'll need energy for when you're not working tonight.'

'I've had emails from Sean.' She shuffled back

against him, and he groaned, squeezing her ribs between his thighs.

'Much more of that and I won't be responsible…'

'We agreed on what we think of responsibility.'

'Mmm. Overrated. So…'

'So I need to deal with them, responsibly, and then…' Her breath stuttered as his lips found the sensitive spot beneath her ear.

'Then?' His inbreath was ragged.

'Then, if you wait here, we can make love under the olive trees.'

'Sophia…' His hand slid under the hem of her tee shirt, spreading across her ribcage.

Taking a deep breath, she tried to focus.

'Sean is excited about that Van Gogh I found. He's contacted a couple of historians, and they're doing more research into it.'

She heard the smile in his voice as he rested his cheek against her hair. 'I have more research of my own to do. And it involves you. Intimately.'

With an effort of will, Sophia dragged her attention back to her work. 'I need to reply to him. The reappearance on the market of a Van Gogh which hasn't been seen for thirty-five years will attract a frenzy of interest.'

Loukas withdrew his hand and smoothed the edge of her tee shirt.

'Yes, I expect it will.'

She felt him shift behind her.

'There'll be a big increase in interest in the sale. There'll probably be a bidding war.'

His dark brows drew together. 'It'll mean more publicity.'

Sophia felt tension stiffen his body, and she thought back to the man she'd encountered when she'd arrived on Alysos: stressed, unsmiling and unwilling to engage with her. She didn't want him to return to that mindset, but she had to be honest.

'It will.' She kept her voice calm. 'At the moment Sean has tried to keep this under wraps, but the interest it will cause is unavoidable, once the information becomes public.'

'I want my name kept out of it.'

His hands rested on his bent knees and she placed hers over them.

'I've repeated that to Sean. The sale will be advertised as the Christos Georgiou collection. But it is his job to generate as much interest in it as possible, to ensure the best result. The inclusion of a Van Gogh, if it's authenticated, will move the interest up a gear. Or five.' She cupped his cheek in her palm. He turned his head and pressed his mouth to the soft skin of her hand. 'But trust me, Loukas. Your privacy will be respected. I promise.'

Loukas lay awake, staring into the darkness. Beside him, Sophia's breathing was light and even, her body warm against his.

He lifted her arm, from where it lay across his

chest, and clasped her hand in his, kissing her fingers. She stirred.

He'd like to wake her and lose himself in her, again. Making love to her stopped him from thinking of anything but her beautiful, responsive body. The words she whispered sent his desire rocketing. It drove the demons that had plagued him for years from his mind, and afterwards he slept the sleep of sated exhaustion.

Except this time, he hadn't. The disquiet that her news about the Van Gogh had raised in him had returned as soon as she'd fallen asleep, and he couldn't shift it.

She'd promised his privacy would be protected, but how much could she really control? What if the press, digging for information about the picture, began asking questions about what happened to Christos, and his godson? And what would happen if it became known that Sophia was Christos's daughter? Privacy would become a distant memory for her. As a wealthy heiress, with a tragic past, she could become the subject of intense media interest. And she would hate it.

He could stop this with a single call to his lawyer. If the ownership of the art was in question, the sale couldn't happen. The promotional campaign hadn't begun yet, and this would mean it never would, but the discovery of the Van Gogh would be big news, whatever the status of the sale. He hoped the historians employed by Marshalls were trustworthy.

'What's wrong, Loukas?' Her voice, slurred with sleep, whispered through the dark.

He shifted, pulling her closer. 'It's okay, sweetheart. Go back to sleep.'

But she moved up, putting her head on his shoulder. 'Do you want to tell me what's bothering you?'

'Mm. It's nothing. Nothing important.'

'It can't be nothing, if it's keeping you awake.'

'Sophia…'

'Are you worried about the sale? The publicity?'

He took a while to order his thoughts.

'Yes,' he said. 'I am.' She placed her hand flat on his chest and he knew she could feel the steady thump of his heart beneath it. 'You've promised to protect my privacy, but how much can you really do?' He pressed his mouth to her temple. 'Other people already know about the painting so it's out of your control.'

'When I get back to London I'll make sure the security is watertight.'

The idea of her leaving sat like a weight on his shoulders. He wanted this perfect existence to go on for ever, just the two of them, not answerable for their actions to anybody else. With his wealth and position he could make that happen, but he knew she couldn't.

She loved her work. She'd fought for the life she had, and she wasn't going to give it up for an invisible existence with a man who was held hostage by the traumas of his youth. And if he shifted the burden of the art collection onto Sophia's shoulders, to save himself the trouble of the auction and the intrusion on his life the publicity would bring, what would it do to her? She'd trusted him intimately. Could he repay that by going against her wishes?

'Do you doubt me, Loukas?'

She pushed herself up on one elbow and he felt the brush of her breast against his side. His body stirred, desire spreading through his veins.

'I… I don't doubt you will do your best.'

He caught the gleam of her eyes in the dark.

'One of the things you told me about…my father…was that he almost always got what he wanted.' She lowered her head, and he felt her forehead resting against his, her hands closing over his upper arms. 'Perhaps I'm like him. I want to keep my promise, and I want…this.'

He smoothed his hands down her back, feeling her satiny skin shiver under his touch. Their lips met tentatively, then, on a sharp inbreath, he took her face in his hands, his need escalating as she drew the sole of her foot up his shin and rested her bent leg across his thighs.

CHAPTER FOURTEEN

'YOU'RE TRESPASSING! Leave before I...'

The sound of voices had made Sophia pause. Anna and Stephanos were not due back until the following day, so who...?

She rose from her chair as she heard Loukas's shout, the fury in his shaking voice turning the blood in her veins to ice.

She ran through the villa, heart pounding, and pulled the heavy oak door open.

Loukas had the man's shirt locked in one fist while the other was drawn back, clenched, at shoulder height. Before he could throw the punch, she threw herself at them.

'Loukas, stop.' She grabbed his arm and tried to prise his fingers open.

'Get out of the way, Sophia. You'll get hurt. This scum...'

The visitor's expression of alarm changed. He looked sly.

'Sophia? Sophia Shaw, right?'

She opened her mouth to reply but Loukas interrupted her. 'What's it to you? Get off this island, now, before I call the police, and by the time they arrive I'll have made you wish you'd never heard of me.' He gave the man a shove, but dropped his arms to his sides, his fists still bunched.

'Who are you?' Sophia kept her hand around Loukas's biceps, feeling them bulge with aggression. 'What do you want?'

'What the hell do you *think* he wants?' he growled. '*Look* at him.'

His ebony eyes burned with anger, his lips compressed into a thin, severe line. Sophia turned her head away from his furious expression to study the man. He'd stepped back a few paces, out of immediate range of any blow Loukas might send his way. He wore the trademark sleeveless khaki jacket and combats of the photojournalist. One of his many pockets held a notebook and pen, and in another she could see the shiny edge of a mobile phone. Lenses and photographic equipment filled the others. A fancy camera hung around his neck.

Sophia's stomach dropped. 'You're…a journalist. What are you doing…?'

'Sounds like I've found what I was looking for, love. He did call you Sophia?' His hand went to his phone, and he pulled it from the pocket, fiddling with the buttons. 'Mind if I ask you a few questions?'

Sophia swallowed hard and tried to relax her throat. It was closing in panic, restricting her breathing. She shook her head. 'Yes, I do mind. Please put that phone away.' She was willing to bet he'd switched it on to record anything they said. 'And leave. Now.'

He stood his ground. 'Am I the first to get here? Come on, give me a scoop. Where's the painting?' He looked round, as if he expected to see it right there, in front of them.

She felt Loukas move but she wasn't quick enough to stop him. He lunged towards the journalist, who took a step back and almost lost his footing at the top of the stairs.

'Go!' His voice was hoarse. 'Now!'

'Okay, okay.' He slid the phone back into its pouch and backed away. 'I'll go. But I'll be back, and there'll be others. Seems Marshalls needs to call a plumber. Block up the leaks, hey, Sophia?' He winked and then retreated down the steps.

Next to her, Sophia could hear Loukas's breath rasping. She turned to him and put a hand on his chest. His heart pumped hard beneath her palm. 'It's okay. He's leaving. You can call the police and ask them...'

He pushed her hand away and stepped back.

'You said my privacy would be protected.' Through his clenched jaw, his voice was a low growl of rage. 'You promised.'

Stunned, Sophia drew a ragged breath. The shocking encounter had made her shake and now it seemed there was some dreadful misunderstanding going on. 'Loukas, yes, I did promise, and I've kept that promise. I have no idea...'

'You said the Van Gogh would increase interest in the sale, and it looks as if it has. Does this have anything to do with you?'

'Loukas, no! Of course not. I don't know who leaked this to the press, but I do know it wasn't me. I know how important your anonymity is. I would never have compromised that, especially not now, after we've...'

'After we've what? Had mind-blowing, no-strings sex? Is that what you were going to say?'

An icy fist closed around her heart, and she tried to hold herself very still. When she answered him, it was in a low, controlled voice, each word a struggle.

'No, Loukas, that wasn't what I was going to say. I was going to say "made love" but I can see now those words would be inappropriate.' Her hand went to her chest, and she pressed it over her thumping heart. 'But I swear to you I didn't tell the press where to find you.'

'He walked up here and asked for you. By name. And he...*winked*...at you. As if you were in some sort of conspiracy together...'

'Loukas, that's how the tabloid press operates. Surely you should know that. He's trying to provoke a response, and...'

Through the fog of her shock and distress, Sophia heard a click. She swung round. The journalist had not left, at all. He'd stopped, two paces down the path, and turned. As she watched, he lowered his camera and gave a wave.

'Great picture of the two of you. Have a nice day.' He started down the track towards the harbour.

'And,' she continued, 'you've given him exactly what he wanted.'

'I didn't tell him anything.'

'You didn't need to. Your reaction spoke volumes. And he'll twist it into any shape that looks like the story his readers hope to read.'

Sophia narrowed her eyes and looked down at the glinting water. A speedboat was tied up at the quayside, where the *Athena* usually lay. In the distance she could see an inter-island ferry making its way from Skiathos to one of the outlying islands, its white superstructure gleaming in the sunlight and a feathery plume of smoke trailing from its funnel.

It was a perfect Aegean morning. The blue and white buildings shone in the crystal clear Greek light, and the sea, benign and calm, stretched into the distance, under its mantle of intense blue. Yet here, on Alysos, where she'd embraced ecstasy and happiness beyond anything she'd ever imagined, the world was crumbling around her. Loukas's words drummed in her head and savaged her heart. How could she convince him that she didn't know how this breach of his privacy had happened?

There was at least one person who did know, and he was rapidly disappearing down the hill towards that boat that would take him out of reach. And he had taken a picture of Loukas. If she could get his camera, she thought wildly, and destroy the picture in it, would Loukas believe her?

Without considering how she was going to accomplish it, she launched herself down the steps, determined to catch up with the man before he reached his boat.

'Sophia! Stop!' She didn't falter for a second in her headlong descent. Loukas watched her go, oblivious to the dangers of the slippery pebbles underfoot and the steepness of the incline. Her sandals were completely unsuitable for the pace she had set herself.

He was almost incoherent with rage, but he didn't want her to injure herself. Regret at his outburst sent guilt licking through him. The appearance of the journalist had completely blindsided him. It was a shocking intrusion of the outside world into the protected and precious bubble he and Sophia had created for themselves, and a brutal reminder of how little control he really had over his life, and hers. If she fell, the trespassing journalist would have even more of a story, and would be unscrupulous enough to take more photographs.

But if she caught up with him? The man was not going to give her anything she wanted. He'd shove her aside, possibly hurt her. Her leg would be tired and unstable, after the way she was abusing it, not favouring it at all as she ran, leaping from rock to rock, deviating from the worn track and taking a more direct, and much less safe, route to the quayside.

She disappeared behind a clump of oleander, and he took a step forward, holding his breath, convinced she must have fallen, but then she reappeared, stumbled, and carried on.

Even in the grip of his fury, a part of him admitted to an admiration for her spirit and determination. He remembered how it had felt to hold her delicate, beautiful body in his arms, so giving and eager. And then he thought of that same body lying still in the stony dust, her damaged leg failing her, another limb possibly fractured, her head bleeding from hitting a rock...

He leapt down the steps and hit the track running, desperate to obliterate that image from his mind.

He closed some of the distance between them, but not enough. Sophia reached the quayside well ahead of him, but the journalist had seen her coming and he was waiting for her. He'd already untied his mooring line, which he held in one hand.

Loukas heard Sophia's voice as she yelled at him. The man raised his camera again as she squared up to him. He could hear her voice in the still air but not her words, but he could see she was pleading with him, her expressive arms and hands lending weight to whatever she was asking.

The man said something, then threw back his head and laughed. She'd be no match for him. He could push her over with one hand. Loukas had no idea what she hoped to achieve by confronting the trespasser, and wondered if she knew, herself. She lunged towards him, making a grab for the camera, but the man fended her off, pushing her away and turning his back. He jumped onto his boat.

Loukas saw Sophia's weak leg buckle under her as she was thrown off balance. She stumbled, tried to save herself, but tripped and fell, hitting her head on an iron bollard and pitching over the side of the stone quay, into the waters of the harbour.

The boat's engine roared. Horrified, Loukas watched the man spin the wheel and heard the throttle open as he gunned the motor and swerved away from the quay. He took the final few steps onto the wharf, frantically searching for Sophia in the water, very afraid that the departing boat had hit her.

Then he saw her. She floundered, her legs kicking weakly, her arms not attempting the strong, sure strokes he knew she was capable of, and she was beginning to slide under the water.

Fear choked him. The terror of his parents' death filled his mind and panic compressed his chest. The water looked so calm, so benign, but it wasn't, at all. It had taken his parents and had wielded its power over him, almost ever since. And now, just as he'd begun to learn how to face his demons and find a measure of peace, it was flexing its muscles again, reminding him he'd never be able to forget what it could do.

If it took Sophia—if he *allowed* it to take her— this memory would eclipse all the others. Sophia had brought him joy. She had trusted him with her innermost fears and he'd willingly accepted that trust, promising himself he'd treasure it.

So the readiness with which he'd leapt to the conclusion that she was to blame for the appearance of the journalist appalled him.

Was this how life would always be? Would he always react with anger, through fear, to the problems that cropped up in daily life on a regular basis?

His wealth and position had enabled his behaviour. He'd used them to isolate himself from the world of emotion and love—the things that made life meaningful and rewarding. He'd been running from them all his life, afraid of exposing himself to more hurt and loss.

Sophia had shown him it was possible to find

happiness and fulfilment, even when life seemed dark and lonely. To be in her arms was to be in ecstasy, and he wanted more of it, but he'd pushed her away, afraid of being hurt, and of hurting her.

Loukas stood, frozen with fear, and recognised that he could choose to accept what was happening, choose to blame the journalist, or he could choose to act to change it. Only he could rescue her. He knew he could swim—Christos had taught him, and he'd told him it was like riding a bicycle. Once learned, you never forgot how to do it.

Sophia's head broke the surface again, as she kicked weakly. Her bright hair, now dark in the water, spread around her. He could change this, if he could make his heavy limbs obey him. The thought of losing her was more terrifying than anything else he'd ever faced. It was unbearable. He thought of the weight of water and how it had haunted him almost all his life, but the idea of it crushing Sophia was much, much worse. He had to save her. She was more precious to him than life itself. When he had her in his arms again, safe, he'd tell her that. And he'd be honest with her this time. He'd tell her the truth.

He dived into the harbour.

Kicking frantically, he forced his head above the water, but he couldn't see her. He gagged on a mouthful of water and caught a glimpse of her hair, as her body was lifted on the swell from the wake of the departing boat. Somehow, he pulled himself towards her. He had to duck his head beneath the surface again to find her, but then, with a superhuman effort, he managed to get his hands under her armpits and drag her upwards.

Sophia's head rolled onto his shoulder. She was heavy in his arms and a wave of panic immobilised him. There was no one else to help. He was in the water with a semi-conscious woman who was the most important thing in the world to him, and he had to get her out.

The closest he'd been to the harbour since returning to the island had been his trip to the beach with Sophia, but he dimly remembered that there was a flight of stone steps built into the harbour wall, where Stephanos usually moored the *Athena*. Shaking his hair out of his stinging eyes, he spotted it and began to drag Sophia towards it.

The ancient steps were slippery, but they continued down below the level of the water, so he could gain a foothold on them. He lifted Sophia out of the water and stumbled onto the quayside. She coughed up some water and collapsed against him.

'Loukas? How did you…? You're all wet.' She drew in a rasping breath and coughed again.

Loukas knelt and held her, rubbing her back and wiping her sodden hair from her face. Gasping for breath, he couldn't speak, but he was happy simply to hold her while his heart calmed down and his lungs stopped burning. Then he picked her up.

'I can walk, Loukas. It's just my head…what happened?' She lifted her fingers to her temple where a purple bruise was already blossoming.

'No, Sophia, you cannot walk. Not now.' He strode towards the track. She felt light and insubstantial, even though in the water she'd felt heavy. 'You banged your head and fell into the harbour. That trespassing journalist didn't even check that you were okay.'

'Oh… I was going to get the camera from him. He took a picture of us.'

'He did,' Loukas agreed, his voice grim. 'When I find out who he is I'll have him charged with trespass and negligence, and anything else that'll stick. But right now, I need to get you back to the house.'

'You can't carry me all the way up the hill. It's too steep. It's too…'

'Just watch me.'

CHAPTER FIFTEEN

THE DOCTOR, summoned from Skiathos and brought by emergency helicopter, snapped his bag closed and looked down at Sophia.

'I've put butterfly stitches and a dressing on the cut and I'm confident that you are not suffering from concussion.' He ran his eyes over her where she sat, dressed in the navy silk robe, on the sofa in her suite. 'If anything changes please don't hesitate to call me back.'

'Thank you.' Sophia held out her hand to him. 'I'm very grateful to you for coming.'

'You've had a shock and will probably need to rest.'

She nodded. 'Please tell Mr Ariti—Loukas— that I'd prefer not to be disturbed.'

She heard his footsteps recede across the terrace and then the low murmur of voices, speaking in Greek. Several minutes later the slow beat of the helicopter reverberated through the still air. She listened as it picked up speed and changed tone as it lifted off the ground down near the harbour. She pushed herself to her feet, making sure she could balance without falling, and went into the bathroom, turning on the shower.

Clean and dry, she climbed onto her bed and lay back against the pillows. She'd thought she was going to drown. Her head had been fuzzy, but she'd been aware of what was happening, just unable to act on it.

Loukas had overcome his fear of water and rescued her. She owed him her life. But it had been his accusation of her that had sent her on the fruitless chase after the journalist in the first place.

She had trusted him and thought he trusted her in return, but she had obviously been very wrong. He'd felt threatened and hit out at the one person he should have known would never have betrayed him. She'd promised to protect his privacy but she might as well have saved her breath because he hadn't believed her.

She ached all over and her head throbbed, but she knew they were things that would get better in a few days. The ache of sadness would take longer.

Loukas felt he was teetering on a knife edge. His thoughts turned in a relentless circle, always returning to the same point. Coffee was probably the last thing he should have, but he made himself a strong cup, anyway, drinking the thick, bitter brew, too hot, at the little table in the courtyard.

He wanted to blame his state of mind on the trauma of the day, but he knew he couldn't. What bothered him were not thoughts of what had happened, or imagining what might have happened.

As he'd stood, immobilised by fear, on the dock, he'd made a promise to himself. Sophia, with her fierce determination and honesty, deserved honesty in return. He'd sworn to tell her the truth, even though she'd want to put as much distance between them as she could.

He knew he had to tell her. He just didn't know how.

It was late afternoon when Sophia walked across the terrace, wearing her blue bikini with her cotton wrap around her shoulders. Loukas was sitting at the table where they usually ate their meals, his dark head bent over his phone.

'What's wrong?' Sophia frowned, pulling out a chair for herself.

'He didn't waste any time.' He pushed his phone across the table, turning it so she could see the screen. 'There's the picture of the two of us, obviously arguing, and another taken on the approach to Alysos. The text identifies us and our location.'

Sophia bent her head over the screen.

Is this where the new Van Gogh is hidden? read the headline.

And, in smaller print, *Godson of Christos Geor-*

giou prepares to sell collection, thirty years after godfather committed suicide.

The caption under the picture identified Loukas and referred to Sophia as 'an employee of Marshalls, the auction house contracted to arrange the sale'.

But is she something more to billionaire Loukas Marcos? it trumpeted.

'I'm sorry, Loukas.' He shifted in his chair and folded his arms across his chest. 'This is exactly what you were afraid would happen, but I know Sean would have demanded discretion from anyone he consulted. When I return to London tomorrow I'll find out what's happened.' She folded her hands in her lap.

He rubbed his palms over his face. 'I'm sorry I accused you of leaking the news to the press. Having him turn up was a shock. My reaction was uncontrolled and out of proportion. I felt threatened and betrayed.'

'I've told you things I've never told anyone else, and discovering the truth about my parents, and that they loved each other, has been the most precious gift. Their love affair was tragic, and I know how painful it was for you to relive those events.' She closed her eyes briefly, blinking back tears. 'But I gave you something, too. I gave you my trust and you might as well have thrown it back in my face, because, when you needed to, you didn't trust me.'

She swiped a hand across her cheeks. 'I grew up in an atmosphere of accusation and blame. For a child, not being able to trust the adults in their life to be honest is frightening and damaging. I learned only to trust myself. I should have remembered that.'

'There's something I need to tell you...'

Sophia sat back in her chair and watched the play of emotions on his stormy countenance. He looked more like the man she'd first met, rather than the man who'd pulled her from the waters of the harbour and saved her life.

'Which is?'

He reached out and slid his phone back across the table. 'I contacted my legal team earlier and explained about your claim to Christos's estate.'

'You cancelled the sale with Marshalls?'

'No, but my lawyer is prepared to cancel it at a word from me.'

Sophia's mind seemed to stop working for a moment as she tried to take in his words. He'd done this without discussing it with her. She'd asked him to give her time to consider the implications of her position, while she completed the catalogue. The idea of suddenly being the beneficiary of Christos's enormous wealth was impossible to comprehend. Her head throbbed and her throat was suddenly parched.

'You did *what*? I asked for time, Loukas, to

absorb the information, and to complete my job here. Why didn't you listen? I don't know if I want all this.' She swept her arm wide in a graceful gesture. 'Give me your lawyer's contact number and I'll tell him.'

'No.'

Sophia stood up but he took her wrist and pulled her back into her chair. She snatched her hand away.

'Don't touch me. This affects me...*fundamentally*. Can't you see that? You said you'd wait. Do my feelings mean absolutely nothing to you?'

'Please sit down, Sophia.' He kept his voice as level as he could. 'There is something I need to tell you. I haven't been honest with you and I want to put that right.'

Sophia put a hand on the back of her chair and stood very still. Then she slowly sat down again, on the edge of it.

'What is it, Loukas?'

'The truth of how I failed Christos.'

CHAPTER SIXTEEN

'WHAT DO YOU MEAN?' Sophia whispered. 'You were only eight. How could you have failed him?'

She gripped her hands together in front of her, but he could see that they shook. Her teeth fastened on her bottom lip and a small bead of blood appeared, shockingly red against her pallor.

He reached out to her, wanting to wipe away the blood with his thumb, but she shrank from his touch. The movement hurt him more than he would have thought possible. He wanted to put his arms around her and hold her close to his heart and tell her he could explain, if she'd only let him.

Would he be able to find the words he'd never spoken to anyone, ever before? Should he?

There was no possibility of going back and he was glad.

'Sophia, let me…'

'What? Let you…what, Loukas?' Her voice trembled, breaking. 'Let you change your story? Why would you want to do that? If the one you told me was a lie, do you think I'm going to believe anything you say? Ever again?'

'I want you to know the truth. I've lived with this in my head…in my *heart*…since that night and it's stopped me from living a proper life. All the wealth and privilege in the world can't compensate for the lack of love, or proper connection to other people. I've let the trauma of my childhood dictate how I've lived my life, but I need to change that if I'm ever going to feel free of it. You deserve to know the truth, and you deserve to be able to be proud to be Christos's daughter and heir.'

'All right,' she whispered, after a long silence. 'Tell me.'

Loukas folded his arms on the edge of the table, shoulders hunched.

'I saw Christos and Helen, as I told you. Alan, your grandfather, pulled Helen away and pushed her behind him. She fell but he left her and turned back to Christos.'

Loukas raised his head, but Sophia remained motionless, staring at the tabletop.

'Go on,' she said.

'Christos had his back to the edge of the cliff and I could see the danger. I wanted to warn him, but I was afraid. Alan had his fists raised but he suddenly dropped them. He said something, and Christos answered, but at that moment Helen called out to him and his attention was distracted.

He tried to go towards her, but Alan put his hands on his chest and Christos disappeared. I heard Helen scream, and that's when I ran away.'

At last, she looked up. Her eyes were dull and opaque, and she wiped her cheeks with the back of a hand. She took a deep breath.

'My grandfather killed Christos.' He'd expected her to react with horror, or at least shock, but her voice was flat. 'Perhaps that explains a lot about his behaviour towards me. He'd been responsible for the death of my father, the man his daughter loved. And I, the result of that love, was the reason she died.' She shook her head, pulling the wrap around herself. 'You must wonder, every day, how things might have been different, but it wasn't your fault. You were a child.'

'I've never told anybody the truth and I intended to keep it that way, until we discovered he was your father. Even then, I couldn't bring myself to tell you. I didn't want to admit to you that I'd failed him. I thought you'd leave at once, and I wanted you to stay.'

'That should have been my choice to make.'

Loukas's shoulders dropped. He pressed his fingers to his forehead.

'Yes, it should, and I apologise. But can you understand why I feel I owe it to Christos to at least make sure you have the opportunity to be the heir to his estate? I believe it's what he would have wanted. I can't change the past, or bring him back, but I can do this to try to put things right.'

'Yes,' she said, 'I understand that. I'm pleased to know the truth. As I mull over it I think quite a lot of the circumstances of my childhood will make more sense. My grandfather must have borne a huge burden of guilt for the rest of his life, and I wonder if my grandmother ever knew?'

She rubbed her palm over her thigh. 'And I hope making the decision to try to break the shackles of your childhood trauma will free you, Loukas. Do you think you'll find a way through this now, to be able to allow yourself to connect with life in a more meaningful way?'

Loukas massaged his temples, trying to ward off the pounding of a headache that was starting up behind them. He forced his voice to be calm, devoid of emotion, although it took a supreme effort of self-control. If by that Sophia meant changing his lifestyle so they could be together, he should be able to do it in a heartbeat. It was what he wanted, from the depths of his soul, but he did not have the courage. He didn't know if he would ever be brave enough to allow himself to be so vulnerable.

'I don't want to,' he lied, unable to meet her direct blue gaze. 'I don't do relationships. I thought you understood that. My lifestyle suits me.'

How could he tell Sophia that he was afraid,

that her fortitude and courage frightened him? She'd lost everything in one cruel twist of fate. She'd known absolute vulnerability, but she hadn't let it stop her building a new and fulfilling life for herself, in which she deserved to find a devoted husband and have a family of her own.

He could not be that man. He'd lost everyone he'd ever loved. How did he know that he wouldn't lose Sophia, too? That she wouldn't break his heart, if he gave it to her?

And what if he broke her heart, if he couldn't make the relationship work? He couldn't bear the idea of hurting her.

'I don't believe you,' she said, eventually. 'I think you're afraid of allowing yourself to be vulnerable, opening yourself to the possibility of being hurt.' She unfolded her legs from underneath her and gathered the cotton wrap around her body. 'But I know that, whatever it is, if you don't confront it, it's going to stop you from leading a life of fulfilment. It's going to stop you from loving. And being able to love someone else, wholeheartedly and without restraint, is one of the greatest gifts in the world.'

'I never mentioned love.'

'Is that because the idea of it scares you? None of us knows what the future holds. If you live your life in fear of what may happen, because of what happened in the past, you'll deny yourself any chance of happiness. If I'd done that I'd be terrified to step out of my front door in case something terrible happened. You said yourself that fear corrodes. Is that really the life you want to live?'

Loukas watched as Sophia rose in a single, graceful movement. She turned, placing a hand on the back of the chair as she swayed, a little off balance. He reached out to steady her, but she stepped back.

He stood up. 'Sophia…'

With an expressive gesture of a hand she dismissed him, shaking her head. 'Sadly, Loukas, as we know, bad things happen in life. Nothing can stop that. But it's how we react to them that's important. I gave you my trust. It wasn't done lightly, and I thought you appreciated that. But when you should have believed in me you couldn't. What we've shared has been very special to me, and I hope it has to you, too, but I think it needs to end, now.'

Then she walked away, poised, her head high, her back straight and her tread light, showing only the slightest trace of a limp.

CHAPTER SEVENTEEN

'WHAT THE HELL HAPPENED?' Sean rose from his chair and planted his fists on the polished surface of the desk. His short silver hair, usually impeccably combed, stood on end. His zebra-striped bow tie, which Sophia knew would match his socks, was crooked, and one of his red braces was twisted.

The eyes that glared at her over the top of half-moon spectacles were steel-grey and angry.

Sophia smoothed a hand over her thigh, a flush of anxiety bumping up her heart rate. Trying to look professional, not like someone who had shattered into a million pieces and put herself back together in the wrong order, she'd tamed her hair into a severe up-style. Now she resisted the urge to check whether it was still in place. Sean was inclined to be irritated by fidgeting. She pushed her hands into the pockets of her skirt.

'I don't know. What happened?'

'You don't *know*?' Sean straightened up and rocked back onto his heels. He removed his glasses, slipped them into his shirt pocket and folded his arms across his chest. 'You come into the office after being closeted on a Greek island for three weeks with...'

'It wasn't as long as that. It was—'

'However long it was, or wasn't, it felt like for ever.' He pointed an index finger at her. 'You come in, on your first day back, looking like you found a Van Gogh but mislaid a Rembrandt, and ask *me* what happened.' He shook his head. 'Give me a break, Sophia.'

'I'm sorry, Sean. I don't understand.' Hidden in her pockets, her fingernails dug into the palms of her hands as she thought she probably understood perfectly. 'I think you need to explain.'

Sean eyed her. He swiped his hands over his face. 'He put the sale on hold. This morning. *That's* what happened.'

Sophia felt as if someone had landed a blow beneath her ribs, knocking the air from her lungs. She pulled her hands free of the pockets and squeezed her forearms across her stomach, trying to remain upright. Her legs felt dangerously unsteady. She'd hoped, all through the long journey the day before, that he wouldn't do anything until she'd had more time to think about what had happened. Perhaps his lawyer had advised him to take this step. He knew to lose the contract would impact on Marshalls, and therefore on her.

'You've gone very white, Sophia.' Sean's voice seemed to come from a long way away, which was strange because suddenly he'd rounded the desk and was next to her, his hands on her shoulders as he pressed her into a chair. 'Put your head between your knees. *Please* don't faint.'

She heard water being poured.

'Here.' He took her hand and folded her fingers around a glass. 'Sip it slowly.'

She uncurled her body and clutched the drink in both hands. Her head slowly stopped spinning as the unnerving, loud buzz in her ears faded.

'Thank you.' She shook her head. 'I'm sorry.'

'Sorry doesn't begin to cut it. Do you know what this means?'

'Yes, I do. Absolutely. You don't need to explain it to me.'

'So now that we're on the same page, can I ask you again? What the hell happened?'

Sophia put the glass on the desk, next to where Sean had propped himself against it. She didn't plan to tell him, or anyone else, exactly what had happened on Alysos. Loukas's story was his, not hers, to repeat, if he chose. And what had happened between them…she couldn't bear to think about it, let alone put it into words, even if she wanted to.

But she'd have to come up with something to satisfy Sean. He was her boss and she owed him an explanation. Did Loukas think she would tell Sean about being Christos's heir? Perhaps this was another example of his inability to trust her, or anyone. By putting the sale on hold he was taking control of the situation. To be secure he needed to be in control.

'Something unexpected came to light. There's a possible dispute over ownership of the collection.'

She glanced down at her hands, gripped together in her lap.

'What?' Sean stared down at her. 'How is that possible? Loukas Ariti inherited it thirty years ago, and *now* someone is disputing the terms of the will?' He swore.

'Also,' she said, anxious to divert Sean's attention from asking who this person making an outrageous claim was, 'on the day I completed the compilation of the catalogue, a journalist managed to get onto the island. It upset Mr Ariti very much. He accused me of tipping off the press about the Van Gogh. He was massively angry.'

'You hadn't, of course.'

'No. I would never have done that. But someone did.'

'I'll look into it. Did he throw you off Alysos? Was he abusive?' Sean's eyes flicked to the bruise on her temple, and Sophia touched it with her fingers.

'Not at all. This was…something else. I left of my own accord. I'd completed the work I went to do. There was no…reason to stay longer.' Her voice cracked and Sean frowned.

'But you had a disagreement. I did see the photograph.'

'We had an argument. Yes.' She blinked rapidly, biting her lip and then remembering she'd bitten it recently. She pressed the back of her hand against it.

'Ah.' Sean's astute gaze softened. He crossed his ankles and placed his hands either side of his hips. 'Was the argument restricted to a discussion about who was responsible for the leak, or was it personal?'

She nodded. 'It was both. It was unprofessional of me to engage on a personal level with a client, and I apologise'

'No need.' One corner of Sean's mouth quirked. 'I'm always telling you to get out more. I can hardly object when you do.'

Sophia thought of the days and nights she and Loukas had spent together, wrapped in each other's arms, their need for each other insatiable. If Sean wanted to describe them as 'getting out more', she wouldn't try to enlighten him. She could never find the words to describe the intensity of what they'd shared.

'It was wrong, nevertheless.' She could apologise, but she couldn't bring herself to regret one single second of their time together.

'But he hurt you. I'm sorry about that.'

'No.'

'Don't deny it, Sophia. I can see an ocean of hurt in your eyes.'

'I think we hurt each other.'

Sean drew in a deep breath. He pushed himself away from the desk and stood looking down at Sophia.

'Would you like me to make a complaint to him? If you think you were unprofessional, he was, too. It takes two to tango, as they say.'

'No, Sean, please don't do anything, although your concern is kind. I'll be fine.'

'Well, you look like hell, Sophia, so maybe you should take a few days off.'

'You really know how to make a girl feel good.'

Sean smiled. 'It's one of my strengths.'

'But I think I'll accept your offer of a few days off. Thank you. It may be best if I'm not involved in the project any further.'

'Maybe. We'll see what happens. If it can be resolved, great. If not, life will go on. It'll be a setback but not a disaster.'

Sophia stared out of her sitting room window, across the road to the Common. A dog raced in circles, chasing leaves, ignoring its owner's calls. The low afternoon sun shone through trees tinged with yellow and gold and she knew if she went out there'd be a chill in the air.

She was lost without her work, and she needed

her brain to be engaged with something that wasn't herself, or Loukas.

As she'd walked away from him she'd realised, with a shock that was devastating, that she loved him. She'd fallen in love with a man who couldn't return her feelings. She'd walked out of his life but at least, she told herself, she'd left with her dignity intact. He'd never allow himself to try to understand her true feelings for him because to do so would be to admit that he cared.

The pain of loss might ease with time, but she knew it would never leave her completely. She reviewed her options for occupying the days ahead. However grim she felt, she had to keep busy, and try to stay positive. It was that attitude that had saved her after the accident, and it would work again, if she believed in it.

She opened her computer and replied to the charity, agreeing to speak at their annual conference. Then she went to her desk and found the keys to her grandparents' house.

Dust sheets covered the furniture but the pictures she remembered from childhood stared down at her from the walls.

None of her memories of this place were happy ones. A sense of loneliness and tragedy seemed to permeate every corner of the building. She'd felt stuck with it, always clinging to the hope that one day, somewhere under its roof, she'd find something that would speak to her of her mother or father.

But now she knew their story. They'd fallen in love and had a passionate affair and the knowledge that she was the result of it gave a value to her life that she'd never considered before. Her father had loved her mother, and her mother had wanted his baby enough to go through with the pregnancy, even though she knew it was dangerous.

She wondered how her grandfather had felt, living with what he'd done, whether it had been deliberate or an accident. Did her mother stand up to him and accuse him of killing Christos? And how had he felt when they were left with Christos's baby to raise?

She'd never discover the answers, but she didn't need to. The house could go because she'd found the connection to her parents she'd wanted. Her tragedy was that she'd lost her heart in the process.

She pulled the dust sheet away from her grandfather's desk and searched through it. In the third drawer she found the bunch of labelled keys and she rattled through them until she found the one she wanted: *Helen's Room.*

Before she could change her mind, she made for the stairs.

The room, on the top floor, had been locked her entire life. Unlocking it and stepping across the threshold felt like a huge transgression against some unexplained law. The ceiling sloped at angles under the eaves and the window looked out over the overgrown back garden.

There was an old-fashioned wardrobe and a dressing table, a hairbrush lying on its surface. She walked across the dusty floor and sat on the edge of the narrow bed. Then she pulled out the drawer of the bedside cabinet, not knowing what she was looking for, but trying to make a connection between this meagre room and what she now knew of her parents: the dashing Christos and fragile Helen.

There was an ancient packet of aspirin, a leather bookmark, and a small silk purse, at the back. With shaking fingers, she eased the zip open and extracted a pale blue envelope, addressed simply to *Helen* in a flamboyant script. As she slid two fragile sheets of paper from it, a small gold object fell into her palm, gleaming with seed pearls. It took a few moments for recognition to dawn. Then she read the letter through the blur of tears.

It was a love letter from Christos. He'd broken the heart pendant in two and folded one half of it into the letter. The two parts would be mended, he said, when he and Helen were reunited.

If Sophia had wanted proof of her parents' love, it was lying in the palm of her hand.

* * *

Loukas squared up to his personal trainer, again, but the man shook his head.

'I don't think so. You'd better finish the session punching the bag.' He nodded to where the leather punchbag hung from the ceiling of the private gym. 'Whatever it is you're trying to get out of your system, take it out on that, not on me.' He turned and walked away, picking up a towel and slinging it around his neck. 'Or,' he said, over his shoulder, 'you could try cooling off in the pool.'

Loukas watched him go, then landed a punch into his own left hand. It hurt, but nothing could touch the pain in his heart.

He missed Sophia. He ached to hold her, feel her mouth against his, her body beneath him. There were things he wanted to talk to her about, places he wanted to show her. He just needed to be with her, to feel complete again. But, wrapped up in his own guilt and self-recrimination, he'd driven her away. He'd said he had no interest in changing his lifestyle and she must think him self-centred and selfish, but the truth was that he was afraid of admitting his feelings. Indulging his own fear of being hurt, he knew he'd hurt her. He'd seen the want in her, the need for him to acknowledge it, and he'd refused.

He'd let her go, alone, back to London, after she'd walked away from him, and he regretted it bitterly. How could he ever hope to persuade her to forgive him and trust him again?

Panicked, he'd agreed with his lawyers that the auction should be delayed, but he should have discussed it with Sophia first. How she was feeling about the enormous possible change in her circumstances.

He doubted she'd reply if he emailed or messaged her and anyway he couldn't put into the words of an email what he wanted to say. He needed to see her.

CHAPTER EIGHTEEN

'WHEN CAN YOU come back in? Or are you having such a good time you're giving up work?'

'If waiting for a removal van is having a good time, then you'll have to be patient while I get over the excitement.' Sophia glanced at her watch. 'They're late, which increases the tension.'

Scan laughed. 'How are you doing, Sophia? At least you're sounding more like you.'

'I'm okay. What's happening?'

'Loukas Ariti wants to discuss the possibility of mounting an exhibition of the collection, if the party disputing the will agrees, while they wait for the issue to be resolved.'

Sophia's stomach went into freefall. She gripped her phone to make sure she didn't send it clattering to the tiled floor and lowered herself onto a chair. When she managed to speak her voice sounded like a stranger's.

'An exhibition? Of everything?'

'Are you okay, Sophia? You sound odd.' Sean didn't wait for an answer. 'Everything except the Aphrodite, apparently. He wants to keep that where it is.'

'He won't want me involved.' She rubbed her fingers across her forehead, wishing the removal van would turn up so she could end this conversation. 'We didn't exactly part on good terms.'

'As I see it, this isn't his decision to make. It's mine. You've catalogued the collection and you know what we're dealing with. We need you on the team.' He paused. 'And besides, he hurt you, so he doesn't get to try to dictate what you work on.'

'What if he withdraws the offer?'

'I'll stand by what I've said.'

'That's very generous, Sean, considering what Marshalls has to lose.' Her mind raced, wondering what Loukas's motive was. Was this so that he could get the collection off the island and out of his way?

The past had held her back for years but putting her grandparents' house on the market had helped her to loosen the bonds it had on her and move forward. She had to find a way to accept there was no future for her with Loukas, however much she loved him, and perhaps engaging in this exhibition, having to deal with him on a professional footing, would help her to begin the process.

If she could take control of her feelings, instead of allowing them to swamp her, she'd have a better chance of controlling her life.

This might be difficult, but she'd do it.

She might love him for ever, but she had to move on.

It had been a chaotic week.

From making the decision to sell her grandparents' house to returning to work had felt like an impossible leap, but she was grateful she'd made it. She felt empowered and positive, able to confront her feelings for Loukas and acknowledge them, rather than trying to deny them. Denial consumed far more energy and required constant vigilance, whereas accepting that she loved him but he couldn't love her back was a fact she would have to learn to accept.

After yet another meeting with Sean and other staff, on Friday afternoon, he asked her to wait.

'He wants a meeting,' he said, without preamble.

'I suppose he does.' She kept her voice level. 'When are you going to Athens?'

Sean leaned back and studied the ceiling. 'The thing is, Sophia, bottom line, he wants a meeting with you. And not in Athens. He's in London.'

She breathed in and dropped her head as she controlled the outward breath. 'I'll be in the office on Monday morning. He can come in and see me then.'

And there'll be people all around me so I won't do something stupid.

'He said he's only here for the weekend. He wants to see you tomorrow.'

'Do you think this is necessary?'

'I don't know. But it's your call, Sophia. I'll support you in whatever you do.'

Sophia chewed her lip. 'Thank you.'

It would be easy to refuse, and probably justified. It felt as if Loukas was being manipulative. But, she thought, he could only manipulate her if she allowed it. Working on this project, she was going to have to see him, and she would feel far stronger if she controlled when that happened.

'All right,' she said, at last. 'You can let him know I'll see him.'

Sean nodded. 'You're sure? He suggested his penthouse at nine-thirty.'

'I'm sure. But not at his penthouse. I'll meet him at a place of my choosing, and at ten o'clock.'

'He said he'll send a car for you if I can give him your address.'

She hesitated. She'd already told him she lived in a flat on Clapham Common. If he really wanted to find her, he probably could. 'Okay. The driver can drop me off and then collect him.'

'Thank you. And if you change your mind, let me know. I'll deal with it.'

On Saturday morning Sophia sat at her desk and composed a note and then she wrapped the half of the pendant in it and addressed the envelope to Loukas. She pulled on jeans and a pale blue sweater. After listening to whatever he had to say, she'd give him the note and go for a long walk. It was safer to put the words she wanted to say down on paper. If she tried to say them she might cry and she wasn't willing to risk that.

She needed to be free of him, to move on with the life she'd been leading before she met him. It could never be the same, but that didn't mean it couldn't be good.

But the thought of a life without him in it felt bleak. She wanted him, with every fibre of her being. If loving someone had to feel like this, she never wanted to love again.

It wasn't worth the pain she carried with her, every hour of the day, the darkest hours of the night when she woke, finding the space next to her cold and empty, or the realisation that came with every morning that she'd walked away from him.

If she'd turned back, that day, and told him she loved him, would it have changed anything? She didn't think so, but she wished she'd tried.

At a minute to ten a black Jaguar with tinted windows drew up opposite her flat. She slung her bag over her shoulder and went to wait by the door, adrenaline already pumping. She released the front door as soon as the intercom buzzed.

Then she breathed out and centred herself, dropping her tense shoulders and lifting her chin.

Footsteps mounted the stairs and stopped outside her door. She twisted the latch and pulled it open.

Sophia stepped backwards, clutching the edge of the door for support.

'May I come in?' Loukas stepped past her, then turned and eased her fingers from the door and closed it quietly. She pulled her hand away and he let it go.

'I was expecting your driver. I thought you'd asked for a meeting...'

'I've told my driver to go and have a coffee. I'll call him.'

'I'm not comfortable with this, Loukas. I think you should go.' She tried to wrest control of the situation, but he stood firm.

'I need to talk to you, Sophia. Please...hear me out. Then I'll leave if you want me to.' He looked round. 'Can we talk through here?'

He walked into Sophia's bright sitting room, glancing over his shoulder to make sure she followed. He frowned. She looked pale, and thinner than he remembered. She gestured towards an armchair.

'Would you like to sit down?'

He shook his head. 'No, thank you. I prefer to stand.' He turned, keeping his back to the wide sash window. 'Sophia...'

He'd rehearsed what he planned to say for days: all the way from Athens on his private jet, all the way here in the car from his penthouse in

Mayfair. But now he couldn't remember any of it and the words beating a tattoo in his brain, as he was confronted by her luminous beauty, were not what he planned to say. Not yet. He was very afraid of scaring her off.

But somehow it seemed being in her presence did strange things to his mind because when he took a deep breath and opened his mouth to speak, the words came out, anyway.

'I love you.'

He heard her soft gasp, but she shook her head.

'Loukas…'

'I love you,' he said again. 'Absolutely and completely. When I'm with you, I believe I can do anything, *face* anything. Your strength makes me strong and your beauty…you take my breath away.'

He dropped his head. 'I have lived my life regretting that I lacked the courage to try to save Christos. When you fell into the harbour, my fear of the water almost stopped me from saving you, but I knew that if I lost you I would not recover from it. And then I let you walk away because asking you to stay would have made me feel too vulnerable. What if you'd refused? What if you agreed, and then I hurt you? I could not find the courage to take that leap into the unknown. Because, for me, love is completely alien territory. It means leaving my place of safety, with no guarantee of finding my way back.'

He took a deep breath. He wanted to cross the space between them and take her in his arms so that she couldn't retreat, but he had to let her do that if she chose. 'You were right when you said I was afraid of opening myself to vulnerability. I decided, aged eight, that I would never trust another person in my life, because trusting someone means they can hurt you and I'd had enough of that.'

'Loukas...'

He held up a hand. 'Please let me finish. I need to say this. I cannot,' he said, with emphasis, 'spend the rest of my life regretting that I did not ask you to stay, that day. I wanted you to, with every cell in my body, but I was afraid. I'd seen how hard it was for you to trust me, and yet I couldn't repay you with trust of my own.'

'And now?' Her voice was quiet. 'What has changed?'

'Changed? Nothing has changed, Sophia. I'm still afraid. I was afraid you'd refuse to see me again. I'm afraid that I've wrecked any chance I have of happiness. I'm afraid you don't love me.'

She took a step forward and braced her hands on the back of an armchair. Her narrow shoulders shook.

'But can't you see, Loukas, that everything has changed?'

He stared at her. 'Do you mean your feelings have changed? Or perhaps I've destroyed them?

I thought what we felt for each other was something extraordinary. But as I said, love is unknown territory for me…'

'No, Loukas, that's not what I mean. Everything has changed because, even though you're afraid, you're here. You've told me you love me, even though you don't know how I feel about you. You've been brave enough to take that leap, to try to escape the things that have held you back for so long.'

'Please just tell me, Sophia, if you think the feelings you had…I think you had…'

'My feelings haven't changed, Loukas. I wrote you a note to tell you, because I didn't trust myself to be able to express them in person. It's in my bag.' She glanced at the floor, where her handbag lay, forgotten as it had slipped from her shoulder. 'I realised in the moment that I walked away from you that I love you, but I didn't have the courage to turn back and admit it.'

Loukas crossed the room in two strides and put his hands on her shoulders, turning her to face him. He folded her in his arms, sealing her body against him, needing to feel every inch of her. He brushed his cheek against her hair, breathing in her scent, moving his hands over her in feverish rediscovery.

'Loukas,' she breathed, 'in your arms is the only place in the world I feel I truly belong. I felt it the first time you held me, when you stopped me from falling on the edge of the pool, and the feeling has only grown stronger,' she whispered. 'When I left you, I felt as if a part of me had remained behind. The world I returned to felt alien and difficult to navigate, without you.'

He guided her to the sofa and pulled her down onto his lap, running a thumb along her cheekbones before tilting her chin up. Their kiss was tentative, at first, as if they were afraid of hurting each other, but she slipped her hand into his hair and angled her mouth across his. He felt her breath quicken as she turned her body to face him, freeing his shirt and placing her hand on the bare skin of his chest, over his thundering heart.

'Sophia...'

'Shh.' She rested her head on his shoulder. 'I found half of the gold pendant. Christos gave it to my mother. They were going to put it back together when they were reunited.'

'Where is it?' He found it difficult to string the words together, as his need for her intensified.

'It's with the note. I was returning it to you.'

'The half he kept was with the photographs. We can repair it so that it's stronger than before, *agape mou*. It will be a symbol of our love.' He dropped his head and claimed her mouth again.

He held Sophia in the circle of his arms, in her bed, his chest rising and falling in a deep and steady rhythm beneath her hand. She turned her head and placed her lips on the skin over his heart.

'Sophia?'

'Mmm?'

'I'd practised what I was going to say to you but seeing you again... It was as though I pressed a "delete" button. I could try to remember...'

Sophia moved her hand to the hard plane of his stomach and laid her cheek on his chest.

'But not if you do that.' He pulled her into his side and captured her hands in both of his. 'After you left, I could barely think or speak. But I managed to call for the helicopter to pick me up. I could not bear to stay on Alysos without you there. In Athens, my lawyer persuaded me the sale had to be put on hold, at least until you'd decided what to do. I wanted to contact you first, but I felt...paralysed.' He paused to kiss her temple. 'The bruise is almost gone.'

She nodded. 'I told myself that the visible bruises would soon heal, but it felt as if the invisible pain would last for ever.'

'Can you ever forgive me for hurting you? I accused you of talking to the press, and as a result you almost drowned.' He kissed her again. 'I intend to spend a lifetime making it up to you. I will never, ever hurt you again.'

She smiled against his mouth. 'A lifetime?'

'Is that too long?'

She shook her head. 'No. But over a lifetime, things will happen, and we'll have to be prepared to face them as best we can. If we trust in each other, any burdens we carry will only be half as heavy.'

'Do you remember saying that the burden of your injury had become the gift of your new career?'

'Mmm.'

'It made me think that Christos would have hated that I viewed his bequest as a burden. I decided that something which had brought us together could not be a burden. That was Christos's gift to both of us. And then I decided to try to get you back.'

'With a speech that you've forgotten.'

He slid his fingers into her hair and caught her chin in his hand. 'Most of it, yes. But the most important words were the ones I said first. They were all that mattered. But if you want to hear them, I can remember the ones that came straight after that.'

'How could you possibly follow an opening line like that?'

'Like this: will you marry me? Please?'

Sophia raised herself on one elbow and looked down at him.

'*Marry* you?'

'Yes, Sophia. Being with you gives me the

courage to love you without restraint. I need you to make me whole and I never want to let you go, ever again.' He swiped tears away from her cheeks with his thumb. 'I've made you cry. I'm sorry. If you need time…'

'I don't need time. I've known almost since we met that I want to be with you, but I was so afraid your past wouldn't allow you to want to be with me.'

He captured her mouth in a long, leisurely kiss, tasting the sweetness he'd missed so much. 'Thank you, *agape mou*. You've helped me to understand that I had to change, or I'd lose you, and you are the most precious, important part of my life.'

Sophia pressed her forehead to his, holding his molten gaze. 'What about Alysos? And the Aphrodite?'

'What would you like to do about Alysos?'

'Alysos will always be our special place. Aphrodite is the goddess of love and beauty and I think she should remain where we found each other, where we fell in love. We'll build new, strong memories there and the old ones will lose their power to hurt. It will always be the place we return to for peace, and to strengthen our love. Our hearts, together, will be strong and safe, just as the gold pendant will be, because our love is unshakeable.'

Loukas felt the beat of his heart accelerate,

strong and true, as she laid her cheek on his chest. He smoothed a hand over the satiny skin of her shoulders and heard her soft intake of breath as he traced the path of her spine with his fingers. He would keep the precious gift of her heart safe for ever, and he knew, with her, he'd found a safe haven for his own.

* * * * *

*If you enjoyed this story
check out these other great reads
from Suzanne Merchant*

Off-Limits Fling with the Billionaire
Their Wildest Safari Dream

Available now!